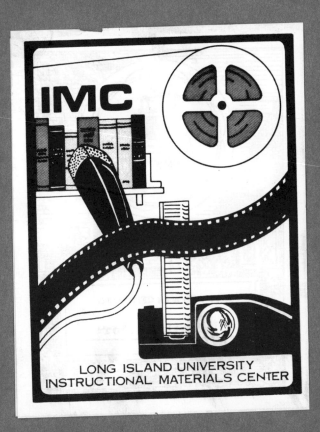

IMC

LONG ISLAND UNIVERSITY
INSTRUCTIONAL MATERIALS CENTER

OTHER BOOKS BY MARY STOLZ:

Wait For Me, Michael
To Tell Your Love
The Organdy Cupcakes
The Sea Gulls Woke Me
Ready or Not
In a Mirror
Pray Love, Remember
Rosemary
The Day and the Way We Met
Hospital Zone
Because of Madeline
Good-By My Shadow
Second Nature
And Love Replied
Some Merry-Go-Round Music
The Beautiful Friend
Who Wants Music on Monday?

A LOVE, OR A SEASON

A LOVE, OR

HARPER & ROW, PUBLISHERS

A SEASON
by Mary Slattery Stolz

New York, Evanston, and London

This book was originally published in somewhat different form under the title TWO BY TWO.

This is for Robert

"Ah, when to the heart of man
  Was it ever less than a treason
To go with the drift of things,
  To yield with a grace to reason,
And bow and accept the end
  Of a love or a season?"

—*Robert Frost*

A LOVE, OR A SEASON

Chapter 1

THE FIRST MORNING TRAIN into Piff's Junction was the 5:11. It left New York at 2:05, an awkward hour for departures, and though it carried baggage, mail, and express deliveries, it took only an occasional passenger.

Therefore Gregg Depew, stationmaster, lifted one brow slightly when he saw young Harry Lynch swing to the platform, suitcase in hand. "Well, Harry," he said. "You're up kind of early. All alone?" He looked about, as though expecting others to materialize at Harry's side.

"Dad and Margaret are driving down on Friday."

1

"And you couldn't wait?"

"That's about it."

Harry put his suitcase down and helped trundle the baggage cart into place beside the open freight-car door. "I'll help with this stuff." He leaped to the cart, greeted the trainmen. Between them they began transferring crates and baggage from the interior of the car.

Old Depew made a motion of protest, then shook his head and leaned against the wagon, watching them. Harry lifted those crates of grapefruit like they were matchboxes. I'm getting old, Gregg thought uneasily. Someday, maybe even someday this summer, all those baskets and boxes and sacks will finally be too much for me. As it was, the trainmen, not saying anything, tried to hoist the heavier stuff for him. And here was young Harry, after either a late night or an early rising, pitching in like it was the most natural thing in the world. Darn nice people, Depew thought, not liking them. It was bitter to find yourself depending on nice people, and even nice people couldn't cover for you forever.

"Here," he said to Harry. "I'll take over now."

Harry only laughed. "Let me, eh, Gregg? Makes me feel of some use to somebody."

Later, in his little office, Gregg fixed them each a cup of coffee. "Use to somebody?" he said. "Boy your age with everything you want. What kind of talk is that?"

Harry stirred his coffee. For a moment, when he looked up, Gregg had the oddest feeling that he was looking not at Harry, the handsome seventeen-year-

2

old who was spending this summer as he had sixteen others in his father's big house on the shore, but at a lonely human being who might have been any age, who didn't know where he stood any more than Gregg did. Then the boy grinned. "I don't know what I meant, Gregg. Thanks for the coffee." Harry stood up.

"You aiming to walk all the way to the Point? If you hang around an hour, there'll be somebody going out that way."

"I like the walk. Across the fields it's less than three miles." It was nearer to seven by car. "Tell you what, though. I could leave my suitcase here till I get a car, okay?" Gregg nodded, and the boy stooped to open his bag, took out a gift-wrapped package.

"Now that looks real pretty," Gregg said with open curiosity. "Who's it for?"

"Nan Gunning, who achieves the good age of sixteen today."

"That right? Little Nan. You kids grow up awful fast," Gregg complained. "So you're taking presents to Nan Gunning these days. What d'you know."

Harry looked briefly annoyed. "Not that way. I've known her forever, and I happened to see a book I thought she'd like. That's all."

"Sort of big for a book, isn't it?"

"Still, that's what it is—a book."

"Okay, Harry. I didn't mean anything." The two stared at each other uncomfortably for a moment. Gregg shoved the suitcase under his desk. "I'll just stow it here," he said. "Any time at all you can come for it."

"Thanks, Gregg. I . . . uh . . ." Harry turned at the door. "Don't pay any attention to me. My best friends find it hard to take these days."

"What hard to take?"

"My company. So long." He was across the road, over the wall, and into the field, heading for the Point and the big Lynch house on the shore. Gregg Depew stood looking after him. Heck of a note, he thought, when a kid who has everything anyone could want goes around feeling sorry for himself that way. Then he remembered that Harry Lynch had lost his mother during the winter. She'd been a lovely-looking woman, pleasant to talk to and generous. But she'd been months dying. Everyone had known for ages that she was going to die soon, so it couldn't have been too great a shock to Harry when, late in the winter, she did. Now it was summer. Think he'd have gotten over it by now, Gregg told himself. Still, you couldn't tell. Some kids took things harder than others. And Harry, the man added determinedly, is as fine a boy as you'd find anywhere. Gregg was a man of simple thoughts, like simple lines impressed in cement and long hardened. He could not adjust to the idea that little Harry Lynch, whom he had once been able to fill with delight by riding him on the baggage cart or treating him to ice cream, who'd been accessible to both teasing and questioning (Gregg was inquisitive, given to raillery), had become a person of unreachable reserves; was, at times, almost a stranger. Following the tall figure as it idled across the first field, Gregg knew a fretful vexation against time that took your

4

strength away and turned youngsters into people even as you watched.

Harry walked slowly, lifting his head now and then to get a deep breath of the sea smell that came across the fields. Salty, seaweedy, fresh as spray, it blew its promise toward him. Lord, how he loved the ocean early in the morning when the long crescent of the beach lay empty and the bright waves folded on the sand. Better than books, better than music . . .

"Look, Dad," he'd said the afternoon before, "why can't we go back today?"

His father had placed a finger in the middle of a long brief and looked up with annoyance. "Back where?" Harry hadn't answered, and Mr. Lynch said, "Oh, to the house. Didn't you ask me that this morning?"

"You didn't answer."

"I was probably busy. I'm busy now, Harry." His glance strayed to the brief, returned to his son. "We'll go back with Warner tomorrow. Or the next day."

"But why? You said we'd go back early this week."

"Harry, I don't have to explain every decision I make. It's simpler this way. Another couple of days won't make any difference to you and they'll make all the difference to me. Besides," he added, "I told you I have to see Collins in the morning. Now, please . . ." His voice and attention trailed off simultaneously; the brief reclaimed him.

"But, Dad, couldn't *I* go? Why do I have to wait while you see Collins?"

Mr. Lynch looked up again. "*Mr.* Collins. We'll say no more about it. You can't," he added, going on to say more about it, "go out there by yourself."

"Mrs. Warner is there."

"Harry!" Harry started out of the library. "Harry?" He turned at the door. "Were you taught to leave a room without excusing yourself?"

"No. Excuse me, sir."

"I'll see you at dinner."

Harry pulled the library door shut, stood in the hall indecisively, then went into the large shaded living room that looked over Central Park. At the window he gazed down where far below traffic moved in an intermittent current. The park was in full summer leaf. It was hot, and even as he stood here among the striped slipcovered chairs and sofas, felt the green broadloom beneath his feet, turned to look thoughtfully at pictures and tables and clocks, he saw the brown-bubbled seaweed waving lazily against the rocks at the Point. His face kept its reflective cast. Margaret, he thought, was going to another party tonight, and his father was seeing Collins tomorrow, so of course they had, or in any case wanted, to stay in town. He, however, was not invited to the party nor required by Mr. Collins. Mrs. Warner was out at the house and could cook for him. Referring to Mrs. Warner had perhaps been a mistake. His father and their housekeeper had for years beyond recall been antagonists, but where Mrs. Warner conducted her offensive in forceful silence, Henry Lynch had more than once been known to yell with rage and was nearly always on the defensive.

"And now, Mrs. Warner," Mr. Lynch had said, shortly after his wife's death, "I think we must have a talk. I don't deny that you've been a great support to us during—" He broke off, rubbing his brow. "However," he'd resumed, "in the future, I think you should have less of a say in . . . in our affairs. That is, the children's. You'll admit that their father *should* have the say, although when my—when Katherine was alive, she . . . needed to feel she could guide them. And when *she* did," he said, his voice rising a little, "that meant *you* did." He paused, but Mrs. Warner's silence drove him on. "I don't wish to hurt you, and certainly I believe you know what value I place on you, but . . . Well, I imagine you understand what I've been saying." He sat back, adjusting his eyeglasses, determined that this time she would speak.

She said, "Warner and I can leave whenever you say."

Henry Lynch got to his feet. "Leave? Warner? What are you talking about? I can't get along without Warner. And I can't," he added desperately, "get along without you." It was true. The slightest fluctuation in his household routine, in his way of life, made Henry miserable, and Mrs. Warner could be relied on to keep it at a minimum. She trained maids expertly, kept intruders at bay, understood the ways of the family, and was absolutely indispensable. He felt he had to have this, the assurance that the furniture would not be changed about, that his children would not have obtrusive problems, that things would not *disturb* him. For this reason he traveled only on business, made no new acquaintances, went out only to places he knew and where he was known. Even his wife had not died with sudden drama, but had somehow contrived to almost make a habit of it. A heartbreaking habit.

"What do you mean, leave?" he demanded now. "Because I make a reasonable suggestion—"

"But, Mr. Lynch, it is not reasonable. I couldn't stop having, as you put it, a say in the children's affairs at this point. We've been together too long. And who would have a say? Could you take over now?"

"I scarcely think you're one to talk. You have no children of your own."

"No," she said quietly. "No, I haven't. But I've helped raise two."

The father of the two subsided into his chair. "I'm . . . sorry. I shouldn't have said that, Mrs. Warner. You're right about Harry and Margaret. Undoubtedly you're right."

Harry had not actually heard this conversation, but the essence of it somehow permeated the house, and while Mrs. Warner, as usual, said nothing, Mr. Lynch let drop an incautious hint or two. "Now, Margaret," he said to his daughter. "Do be tactful with Mrs. Warner. You know, make her feel . . . needed."

Margaret and Harry had looked up in surprise.

"Well, Dad," Margaret said, "that would be sort of coals-to-Newcastley, wouldn't it? Aggie knows we couldn't function twelve hours without her. I don't

8

see the point to up and announcing it." She looked at her father closely. "And why should we? Is something wrong?"

"No, no. Why do you immediately assume something's wrong because I make a suggestion?"

"Because it's a funny suggestion."

"We'll forget I said anything." Mr. Lynch left the room.

His children exchanged a glance. "Sounds to me," Harry said, "as though he and Aggie have been having a dust-up. You don't think she wants to leave?"

"Of course not. And especially not at this time."

Harry closed his eyes. Margaret, his father, they were both able to refer in this way to the fact of Katherine Lynch's death. "When Mother was alive," Margaret would say. And, "Before my wife's final illness," Mr. Lynch would preface a remark. They seemed actually to find comfort in this. Harry could not yet mention his mother at all. He tried not to think of her, never went near the front bedroom, which had been hers, listened to no music and read nothing that reminded him of what they used to share. "It's almost," Margaret had said once, "as if you were trying to pretend she'd never lived." Harry supposed that in her love and concern she was trying to shock him into speaking. He had not answered.

Still, by the summer afternoon when he stood at the window and rebelled at having to remain in town, the muteness of his pain had somewhat passed, and he too could say once in a while, "Mother used to think . . ." He had thought when she died that the loss was not,

9

could not be, bearable. Yet he had borne it, bore it every day. He had believed, because the house on the shore was to her, as to him, dearer than any other place in the world, that he would not be able to go down this year. But they had been there a month now, and this trip to town, senselessly forced on him, who had no business here, was only torment. His father had been coming down weekends, which was customary, and had somehow convinced them on Sunday that a family return to the city was necessary because Margaret's birthday was on Tuesday.

"Why couldn't you stay here instead?" Harry had asked. "Why should we all have to traipse off to town just because—"

"Even if you have no family feeling, you could pretend for your sister's sake that you have."

"Margaret doesn't give a darn. Besides, since it's birthdays we're talking about, it's Nan Gunning's birthday on Thursday. I'd sort of like to be here for that, and if I go in with you, I suppose you won't want to come back till the weekend."

"Nan Gunning's birthday can't be that important to you."

That, Harry realized, was quite true. On the other hand, Margaret's birthday was not important either. She'd be off with her friends day and night, and he'd probably have to shout his felicitations as she went out the door. "I bet if you ask Margaret," he began, "she'd tell you she'd rather have me stay—"

"Harry, will you stop pestering me. Anybody listening would think you were eight years old."

The way I get pushed around, Harry thought glumly, they sure would.

And duly on Monday morning, with Warner at the wheel, they had driven as a family to the city. Mr. Lynch read the papers all the way in. Margaret slept. Harry looked out the window. "Well," he said as they rolled up Fifth Avenue to the apartment, "when's the party?"

Margaret woke with a yawn. Mr. Lynch nested the *Tribune* carefully within the *Times,* looked at the avenue with approval, as though it had been well taken care of during his absence. "What party?" he said.

"I'm going to the Hirsches' tonight," Margaret said. "Only it isn't really a party."

"Margaret's birthday party," Harry insisted. "What we came in for."

"Harry," Mr. Lynch said ominously, "you're being difficult. I did not say at any time that a party was planned. I merely feel that it would be good for the family to be together at times of . . . festivity."

"We'll all be home together tomorrow?"

Henry Lynch leaned across his daughter and eyed his son. "I will go to my office," he said slowly, "as I always do. To earn, I might add, though I shouldn't have to, the money to keep you in school and Margaret in clothes, the money to keep that ark at the shore, among other things. Now have you any questions?"

"No. I just wondered what we were going to do tomorrow."

Margaret looked from one to the other, hunched

her shoulders a little because her father was squeezing her, and said, "I have a date with Richard tomorrow. Tonight, too, for that matter. He's taking me to the Hirsches'."

Mr. Lynch slapped his papers angrily to the floor. "You do not have a date with Richard tomorrow. You have a date with me and your brother. I'm taking the two of you to dinner, and that's final, understand?"

Harry felt a sudden wrench of pity for his father, and Margaret said gently, "Why sure, Dad. That would be awfully nice."

But you can't, Harry thought, standing at the window on Wednesday afternoon, really go on feeling sorry for Dad, because he's insulated against all emotion, including sympathy. They'd had dinner at the Yale Club under a sense of pressure that kept them chewing at top speed. Mr. Lynch did not approve of dawdling. You had to eat, but you did it with efficiency and a minimum of conversation. He himself had a delicate stomach and ate sparingly. It was obviously irksome to watch his two children at their rich meals. Once Harry glanced at Margaret eating away rapidly, like a pretty rabbit, and burst into laughter. His father winced. *Semper inconspicuous,* Harry thought. We could print it on his letterhead. The funny part was that the three of them really were terribly conspicuous, what with his father saying nothing and him and Margaret gobbling like a pair of mendicants. For a moment, as the dessert came in, he toyed with the notion of singing *Happy Birthday, dear Margaret. . . .* Oh, *brother.*

He turned now from the living room window as Margaret came in with Richard. Margaret looked fresh and ruffly as a flower, and Richard, as usual, like a carriage-trade Everyman.

"Hi, sweetie," Margaret said in her slow private-school drawl. "What in the world are you doing?"

"Nothing. Absolutely, literally, nothing. Hullo, Richard."

"Greetings, Harry. Why so glum?"

Harry lifted his shoulders a little. There was about his sister and this latest conquest a sort of sparkle, a *twoness* that excluded, except in words, anyone but themselves; and saying "Why so glum?" to outsiders didn't alter the essential fact that they were together and they were not glum. And nobody, thought Harry, is fooled for a minute. "Look, Margaret," he said, "can you see any reason at all why I shouldn't go down to the Point today? I mean, what the devil am I supposed to hang around here for?"

"Well, darling, if Dad says it's all right, certainly I wouldn't interfere. I think it's a good idea."

"But he doesn't say it's all right. We're going back as a family unit, tomorrow or the next day or whenever we get around to it. As if a day here or there didn't mean a thing. What am I supposed to do around here?"

"Did you ask him?"

"Of course I did. He shooed me away as if I were a kid."

"Harry, you are only seventeen. I mean, parents do still sort of look out for seventeen-year-olds."

"I'm not asking permission to go out on the town and have a high old time. I'm trying to get down to the seashore with a nice respectable old housekeeper, that's all."

"You don't have to jump all over me just because you're mad at Dad."

"I'm just pointing out the incredible inequity of the thing."

"Inequity," said Richard, "is never incredible. It's the rule."

Harry moved impatiently. These men of Margaret's always had to poke their oars in. Margaret seemed to think they were only showing insight, and what, without being rude, could you do about it? There had been a time when Margaret would have shared with him the bitter disappointment of being kept away from the Point for no reason at all. A time, less long ago, when she would at least have understood his disappointment. Now she looked at him with a gay absent-mindedness and right before his eyes forgot what he'd been talking about.

"Richard's vacation starts next week and he's going to come out and spend the *entire* time with us. Isn't that absolutely marvelous?"

"Oh, now, Margaret." Richard laughed.

Harry said, "Yeah. Yeah, that's great. Glad to have you, Richard." In a pig's eye, he told the two of them silently. Richard was an architect (all Margaret's young men were architects or lawyers) and so far as Harry could make out had no opinions on anything. He seemed to perform in an unexceptional middle position, and his strength, Harry thought, lay in an ability to level out the conversation of any company he was in. You couldn't talk about music because Richard only knew what he liked, or about art because Richard only knew what he didn't like. He seemed unwilling to talk about the human situation of the world, found war and politics distasteful, and apparently forgot what the book was about the moment he closed it. So Richard was to spend the entire time with them, was he? Harry wondered how long the entire time was to be.

"I'm going out for a while," he said to Margaret.

"Oh? Where?"

"Just out."

"I suppose I ought to know where you're going," she said doubtfully. "Or, anyway, when you'll be back."

"I'll be back in time for dinner."

"Lambie, I won't be here. Richard and I are due at some fracas in Greenwich."

"Then I'll have to eat without you."

"Harry, what's the matter with you?"

"Oh, let the kid alone," Richard said, and her attention returned to him.

Harry gave them a half wave and left the apartment. On the street he paused uncertainly, as he had in the hall after leaving his father. He could, he supposed, walk over to the zoo or up to the museum. He could walk through the park and watch the kids sail their boats. He could go somewhere and listen to records, maybe buy one if he had the money. He pulled out his wallet. Ten dollars. That was plenty. He began to walk downtown. There was always enough to do in New York. Music to hear, things to look at. But he kept seeing the ocean spread on the pale sand, thinking of the way small shells scuttled under water as the waves went out. He kept hearing the drumroll breakers crash against the offshore reefs. New York was a city on the ocean, but you'd never believe it as you walked this avenue. The ocean by its nature was all curves and rolls and crescents. The city was verticals and horizontals. Even the sun had to angle to reach the streets. The air was hot and breathless. Not a notion of the sea reached it. He walked, hands in his pockets, eyes reflective, and at some point, scarcely noticing, boarded a downtown bus. The windows were open, creating a hot breeze that was not refreshing but did at any rate stir the air. In a sort of lethargy he sat and watched the streets go by. It was interesting to see how at Thirty-fourth the entire character of Fifth Avenue altered as decisively as the blue and green waters of the Gulf Stream were said to—meeting in a line, not blending. Sadder and shabbier the streets and the people grew as they went downtown. And then just as suddenly, at Twelfth Street, mellow, comelier than anything uptown. He got off when he realized the bus was about to start a return trip.

Washington Square was a medley of rich and poor. Nursemaids with veils wheeled expensive perambulators past urchins who, by the age of five, were more or less on their own. Old men played checkers or dozed or simply stared, trying to remember, to forget. Students from the university summer school strolled, studied, flirted. A photographer was taking interesting angles of the arch. There was an artist with an easel and oil paints and an artist with drawing board and charcoal. Harry stopped briefly to watch the oil progress. It had been done a thousand times, this painting. Bit of the arch, a drinking fountain, child with hoop, feathery trees. The artist, old, thready, bright of eye, turned and looked hopefully into Harry's face. Harry studied the canvas, trying to think of a remark that would neither hurt the artist nor insult his intelligence. There was something, perhaps, not quite so trite as the usual "Washington Square—Summer Afternoon." A . . . what? "It has a sort of . . . luminosity," he said finally.

The artist smiled. "I'm trying to get that sort of bronze feeling of the sun in the city." He too regarded the canvas for a long moment. "I don't know. In the end they always look like bad copies of Renoirs that turn out not to have been done by Renoir." He didn't seem downcast.

Harry smiled. "Was there really a child with a hoop around here?"

"No. He had a space gun, or whatyoucallem. But I like hoops. They have a motion of their own, even when they're perfectly still. Balls have too. But not space guns." He leaned forward and added a stroke to the base of the drinking fountain. Then he indicated the grass beside him. "Sit down," he invited.

Harry settled beside the paintbox, examined with

17

enjoyment the squeezed, pungent-smelling tubes. Cadmium yellow, vermilion, burnt sienna, rose madder. No wonder people liked to paint. The thought led naturally to Nan Gunning. It was true that he didn't much care about being at the Point for her birthday, but on the other hand it would be sort of nice to take her a present, even if a couple of days late. Not paints, because she already had so much and he wouldn't know what she really needed. Besides, she was concentrating on drawing this summer, as Harry knew to his discomfort. He seemed to be pressed into unwilling service as a model more often than any of her other victims. Probably because he had more leisure. The Gunnings did not have help, so Mrs. Gunning was usually too busy to sit for hours while Nan caught "that marvelous line of the neck and shoulder—and, Mom, couldn't you lean forward just a little so that your arm sort of embraces the salad bowl?" "Nan," her mother would reply, "no working cook embraces the salad bowl with her arm." "But the line, the *line*." "But the dinner, the *dinner*." Harry grinned to himself. It went on all the time, Nan's wheedling and cajoling for the line, the line.

"What would you buy," he said to the artist, "for a sixteen-year-old girl who likes to paint? For a birthday present."

"Some good brushes."

"She has lots of equipment. Anyway, she seems to be more interested in drawing than in painting at the moment. Grease pencils and all that."

"Wise girl." The artist uncorked a small bottle of

turpentine, swirled his brush in it, wiped the brush on a brilliant shred of rag. "How much do you plan to spend?"

Harry thought about the record he wanted to buy. "About five dollars," he said.

"Why not a nice book? You could go over here to one of the secondhand stores, and if you took your time you might find a real nice book for five dollars. Book on art," he added, as if there might be some question.

"That's an idea," Harry said. "Maybe some Daumier drawings, something like that."

"For a sixteen-year-old girl?" The artist shook his head. "No, no, that won't do at all. You look around for a nice copy of . . . Botticelli, that's it. Perfect for a girl like that." He seemed to have decided for himself what Nan was like. "Yup, Botticelli would be it."

"But that would be mostly paintings, wouldn't it?"

"The drawing, my boy, is there. Those marvelous curls—the details of the landscapes—those flowers. The grace, the delicacy of the lines. And the sureness. Wonderful, wonderful . . ." He scratched his chin, his hand hovered over the paint tubes, he picked up an ultramarine, dropped it, selected a cobalt blue and squeezed a little tendril on his palette. "You won't mind if I continue? The light, you know."

"I have to go along anyway," Harry said, getting up. "Thanks a lot for the advice."

"Think nothing of it," said the artist, but he had already, Harry could see, withdrawn from the larger Washington Square with its talkative strangers to the smaller one upon which he could superimpose hoops because he liked them. Harry took a final look at the canvas from a distance. It really wasn't very good, but he still thought it had something. So amiable, so without misgiving.

In the third bookstore he found the book. Large and old but in good condition. It had fourteen magnificent color plates, about eighty black-and-white details, including some of the drawings for Dante's *Divine Comedy*. Altogether a terrific buy. Glancing through it, stopping here and there to study a plate, Harry saw what the artist in the square had meant. There was so much tenderness and beauty here. Such a sort of twining elegance of line. He paid seven dollars, which put the record out of reach for the time, but it was worth it. There ought to be some tissue paper and ribbon around the house. He would wrap it up nicely, and he bet Nan would be bowled over. If I ever get out there to give it to her, he thought, reverting to his former mood of discontent. It was now nearly five o'clock, and he was getting hungry.

He found the maid, Nora, reading in the kitchen. She put the magazine aside when he came in and smiled at him.

"Hi, Nora," he greeted her. "Where's Dad?"

"It's Wednesday night, Harry."

"Wednes— You mean he went to the club for dinner again? We had dinner there last night."

"Still, it's Wednesday night," she repeated.

Harry shook his head. Worlds could topple and new worlds arise, but on Wednesday night Henry Lynch took dinner at the Yale Club. "Well," he said, "is there anything around that I could eat?"

"Sure, Harry. I'll get it ready for you in no time. Would you mind clearing up after, though? I want to get home as soon as I can."

"Tell me what there is and I'll do it myself," Harry said. "You don't have to stick around."

"Well—" she said doubtfully. Mrs. Warner would not approve.

"We'll keep the hideous secret between us," Harry told her. "Threats of death won't drag it out of me."

"In that case," Nora said, "come on, and I'll get you started."

After she'd gone, Harry put back the double boilers and frying pans, sat down to cold meat, cold string beans (he debated cold potatoes, returned them to the refrigerator), bread, and pie. It tasted all right. He took an apple, wandered into the living room, turned on a lamp, and sat down. Very well, he thought. He repeated it aloud. "Very well." He recognized that he was being ridiculous. There were any number of things he could do. Call someone. Go to a movie. Go up to the Lewisohn. But no . . . he was going to sit in a dimly lit room, proving that he was neglected. Drag you down to the city, he thought, and then go off and leave you alone the whole time. What about all this family closeness he's been force-feeding us for days? Nice game of chess at the Yale Club, nice suburban brawl in Connecticut, nice empty living room on Fifth. Phooey. You could reassemble smashed atoms easier than you could make a close family out of Margaret and him and Dad. Idly he drew the Botticelli toward him and began to leaf through the plates. It was strange how every once in a while this glorious painter could be positively repellent. Some of the Madonna and Child groups he didn't like at all. The "Holofernes" gave him the creeps. And this one—"Mars and Venus." Of course, it was in black and white, so you missed the colors. Everything was marvelously put down—the lines of the limbs, the helmet, the material of Venus's clothes. But the cupids were grotesque, and Mars looked plain stupid, lying there with his mouth open. He looked drunk. Venus seemed sullenly disappointed, as what woman wouldn't be, stuck with this ungodlike Mars? But then you had only to turn the page to find the beautiful "Primavera," the enchanted picture in the forest. Flora, like a figure in a brocade, with her sweet dreamy smile and her falling flowers; these dancing Graces with their tumbling hair; Mercury absently poking in the leaves. All so artificial and so real, so radiant. And "The Annunciation." He looked longest at that, studying the turn of the Virgin's body, humble, full of dignity and grace, as she half bowed to the kneeling angel. These were musical paintings, he thought. They sang.

Yes, he had made a very good buy. He closed the book and got up to search for ribbon and tissue paper, which finally turned up in the sewing room. When he had the package wrapped, he put it in his suitcase, already packed, put the suitcase on his bed, and again took a stand before a window. No one could deny New York its aspects of peculiar beauty. It lay now, filled with night, checkered with golden irregular frets, seamed with moving lights, with still lights. Here the buildings were piled like dominoes with glowing pips, there the shallows lay, pitchy and strange. And over it sailed the sky with its unteachable riddles, its vast uncaring comment. The sea or the city, today or tomorrow, it does not matter.

By eleven o'clock he had taken a shower, read a little, listened to some music. He was lying down, hands beneath his head, feet propped on the sofa arm, when his father came in. He pulled about slowly and got to his feet.

"All alone?" said Henry Lynch.

Harry nodded and then said, "Yes, sir."

"Hmm. I forgot Margaret was going out." Harry wanted to ask whether that would have made any difference in Wednesday night. "What have you done all day?" his father inquired.

"Nothing much. Wandered around."

"Nora fix you a good dinner?"

"Fine."

Mr. Lynch half turned away toward his bedroom. "By the way, Harry," he said, not quite looking around, "Warner's brother in the Bronx is ill."

Even as he guessed what was probably coming, Harry couldn't prevent a little smile. Warner's brother in the Bronx had been a sort of joke among Margaret, his mother, and him. Harry, when he was small, had thought it was all one word. Warner didn't have any other brothers, and everyone had long since located the existing one in the correct borough, but Warner went right on referring to his brother in the Bronx. "I just hope he doesn't move," Katherine Lynch had said once. "No one, including Warner, would be able to identify him."

"And so," Henry Lynch continued, "I told him he could stay off till Friday. We'll start Friday at noon."

"I see."

"Is that all you have to say?"

"I guess so. Oh, I'm sorry about his brother in the Bronx."

Mr. Lynch looked at his son thoughtfully. "I know you're disappointed. But we have to think of other people. Not only of ourselves."

That so? Harry thought coldly. He said nothing.

"Well . . ." Mr. Lynch seemed uncertain and, as a result, irritable. "We might as well go to bed now that that's settled. Good night, Harry." He went down the hall, not waiting for a reply. Harry heard the bedroom door close. Even then he waited a while in the living room, thinking that it was surely probable, or anyway possible, that his father would come out and say, Look here, Harry, there's no reason for you to hang around here. Take the early train down tomorrow and we'll see you on the weekend. But his father's door remained closed, and when at length Harry looked down the hall, there was no light showing through the cracks.

Another fifteen minutes passed before he went to the front door, adjusted the latch, and rang the elevator bell. He tapped his foot calmly to disguise from himself the uncomfortable motion of his heart. Golly, he thought, I wonder how people become burglars or

24

spies. Why aren't they scared to death? The elevator doors slid back smoothly and the face of Frank, the night man, appeared. "You going out at this hour, Harry?"

"Depends on you," Harry said nervously.

"I don't get it."

"Look, Frank, lend me ten dollars, will you?" The elevator man looked astounded. "I'll send it to you, special delivery, tomorrow. As soon as I can borrow it from Mrs. Warner."

"Boy, you're just asking for trouble," Frank said, but his hand went to his pocket, and he pulled out his wallet. "You eloping? Or running away to sea?"

"You might call it running away to sea," Harry said, taking the bill with unsteady fingers.

"Hey, wait a minute," Frank said. "You give me back that money. I'm not gonna be party to—"

"No, no," Harry said. "I was joking. I'm going down to the Point, that's all. I don't have enough for train fair."

"Can't your old man give it to you?"

"He doesn't know I'm going. I mean he's asleep, and I don't want to disturb him."

Frank began to be reluctant. "I don't know, Harry. I mean, suppose your father finds out I had a hand in this. He'd—" Imagination failed. "I don't know," he repeated.

"You don't come into it at all," Harry said loudly. He lowered his voice. "You'll be off when Dad comes down in the morning, and if he says anything tomorrow, all you say is sure you took me down with a suitcase. Are you supposed to cross-examine everyone who rides this crate?"

"Okay, okay, relax," Frank said. "None of my business anyway."

"Now you just wait here," Harry instructed him. "Just let me get my bag." He let himself back into the apartment, stood a moment listening to the stillness, and went cautiously down the hall to his room. Getting his bag and switching off his light was a second's work. He readjusted the latch and got into the elevator with a sigh. As they sped smoothly downward he said, "One other thing, Frank."

"Yeah?"

"When my sister comes in, don't say anything to her about me."

"When your sister comes in, I'll be too sleepy to say anything about anything." He released the doors on the first floor. "You take it easy now," he said in a worried tone. "You sure you're going straight out there? No stops on the way?"

"Believe me, I won't stop till I get there."

He slept for a while on the train, woke at dawn, and with his elbow on the sill, chin in his hand, watched the farmlands go by. He felt peaceful, happy, not at all alarmed. This was the first time he'd ever openly defied his father. He was rather sorry about that and wasn't looking forward to the outcome with much pleasure. But he had done what he had to do. There was an extraordinary tranquility in that.

The sun hadn't risen yet, and in the fields going slowly past, the cattle were only shapes that might have been stones or bushes, except that they moved their jaws from side to side and turned their heads. Two cows stood close to the tracks at one point. They were unalarmed. One had knobby horns and the other a star on her forehead. The houses lay still in their wooden sleep, wet webs swung on the fence rails, mist curled over the ground like Indian pipe. In a meadow a tethered goat slept with his beard in the grass. Gradually the eastern sky began to lighten, pale at first as green grapes, then pink and gold, finally blue and pure and high.

The train pulled into Piff's Junction at five-thirty. It was the five-eleven, so that was pretty good time, Harry thought, swinging to the platform. There was old Gregg Depew, advancing with pathetic courage upon the baggage car. Harry dropped his suitcase and went to lend a hand. He felt a sudden wild surge of strength—in his back, in his arms. He felt like picking up the whole baggage car with one hand, and the trainman and Gregg too. He'd had only a couple of hours of sleep, but he was *here,* and he thought it very likely he'd never need to sleep again.

Gregg fixed him some coffee and began that artless prying and poking which led so many people to tell him their secrets, either from inattention or an exasperated desire to get away. As a child Harry had been an uneasy victim of Gregg's kindliness and curiosity. How, the small Harry had thought, could you accept Gregg's favors—the ice cream cones, the rides on the delivery truck—without answering the things he asked you? "Who's that young fellow out to your house these days?" Gregg would ask. Harry would look at him doubtfully. "Just a guy we know," he'd evade. "*Who* knows?" Gregg would persist. "All of you? Friend of the family?" "Well, sort of, I guess. I mean," he'd stumble on, beneath the spell of Gregg's sharp eyes, "Margaret invited him, but—" "Seems like Margaret's a little young for that sort of thing," Gregg would say decisively. Harry, ashamed, but under an obligation, would mutter that Margaret was fourteen, and anyhow . . .

Yet the day had come when Harry could turn aside the question, and turn it aside again, and their relationship, which had never been friendship but had had a sort of heartiness, declined till it existed chiefly in recollection. Harry, going out the station door, forgot Gregg immediately. Gregg watched Harry only to repine.

The three miles were nothing. There were the fields with their rough grass and wildflowers and bees working so early, wearing their wings away in devotion to a cause. There were the tall trees, nobly, apparently endlessly, at prime; the little trees grimly surviving. There was the warm clovered air giving way to the salt-laced air; and the long *Cooeee* of a farmer calling cows; and a little brown fox streaking across a wall. There was, finally, the sea.

Harry stood at the summit of a steep sand bank clutched here and there by wind-bent evergreens, and for a long time simply looked at what lay before him —the limitless, luminous lifting waters moving serenely under the morning light.

Chapter 2

N<small>AN</small> <small>GUNNING</small>, lying in bed, tried to analyze the character of the light this morning. Not brilliant. It had a sort of softness, a diffused almond color, like sun going through a goldfish bowl. The moving leaves of the oak at her window sifted sun with shape and threw flights of shadow across her wall. It looked very Japanese. A Hiroshige's brush could catch that sense of the leaves—caught, but forever escaping. I wouldn't dare try, she thought.

"Come on in, Mom," she answered to a knock at the door.

"Happy birthday," said her mother. "Does anything feel different?"

"Nothing. Sixteen isn't much. I mean, eighteen—now that would be worthwhile. Or perhaps even seventeen. But you might as well be fifteen as sixteen to my way of thinking. Consider it yourself. Where's the challenge of sixteen? The *hors de combat?*"

Her mother laughed. *"Hors de combat* doesn't mean challenge. It means you're out of the thing."

"My point exactly," said Nan, sitting up. "What time is it?"

"Nearly seven."

"What are you doing up so early?"

"Well, I thought since it was your birthday, *I'd* get breakfast. And since you get up at such fantastic hours . . ."

"I can't imagine a nicer present. Pure devotion."

"Speaking of that—presents, not devotion—wait a second." Her mother went into the hall, returned carrying a tall, narrow, clumsily wrapped package with a weary blue bow sagging at the tip. As Nan bounded from the bed Mrs. Gunning complained gently that why some people could make photogenic packages and others could not was a puzzle to her. "All it is is tissue paper and ribbon. You'd think any competent person could cope with those, wouldn't you?"

"Hush," said Nan, ripping away the sad wrappings. She drew a long, contented breath, then leaned forward and kissed her mother's cheek. "It couldn't be more wonderful."

"It does look sort of professional, doesn't it? Put something on it."

Nan carefully set up the easel, running her hand over the grainy wood. She got a large drawing board, adjusted the bracket, put the board in place, and stood back to survey it.

"I'm a perfectly happy person," Nan said. "What a thing to discover on your birthday."

They looked at each other in silence for a moment before Nan sighed and said, "Well, I probably ought to get dressed."

"How about popovers?"

"Oh, swell," said Nan.

She was on her third popover, her mother on a second cup of coffee, when steps on the gravel of the side path announced a visitor, and there was Harry Lynch at the screen door. He wore shorts, a striped T-shirt, and carried a tennis racket and a package under his arm. "Tennis, anyone?" he said, and let himself in.

"What are you doing here?" said Nan and her mother together.

"Nothing like getting back to your friends. Nothing like the warm spontaneity of the greetings, the sudden lighting of their eyes as they think, Can it be? Yes, yes, it is, it is—Harry, come back again. Nothing like—"

"But you weren't supposed to come back till later. Did your father change his mind?" Nan asked.

"Would you like a popover?" said Mrs. Gunning.

"I'd love one," Harry said, putting his racket and package on the sideboard, grinning because Nan was trying to pretend she did not see the package. "And no, my father didn't change his mind. I did." He put jam on a popover. "There's going to be the devil to pay when he finds out."

"What do you mean?" Nan's mother asked.

Harry shook his head. "I just up and left last night. I saw no darn point at all to hanging around the apartment while Dad and Margaret conducted their affairs. So I borrowed ten dollars from the elevator man and came down on this morning's train. I wish I'd left a note, but I didn't think of it. Don't suppose it would have helped much anyway."

"Oh, Harry," said Mrs. Gunning. "That was an awful thing to do."

"Do you really think so?" Harry asked curiously. "That is—really? Can you tell me why, aside from the fact that my father said so, I should have stayed there, when he knows what it means to me to be here?"

"But you can't just think of what things mean to you."

"Let me put it this way. From the time we got to the city, except for a quick dinner at the Yale Club, the only person I saw was Nora, and she always wanted to get home early. I catalogued some of my records, hung around the apartment, called a couple of guys who were out of town, shared the aforementioned dinner, and rode and walked around the city. I was not required as company for anybody. They were doing what they wanted. Why shouldn't I do what I want?"

"I don't know what to say, Harry. Couldn't you have asked your father?"

"I did ask him, Mrs. Gunning. He said No."

"Oh, boy, he is going to be wild," Nan muttered.

"Have you seen Mrs. Warner yet?" Mrs. Gunning asked.

"Sure. She gave me breakfast. And I had to get the ten dollars from her to send to Frank. I thought you," he said to Nan, "could ride in to the post office with me." Nan nodded. "Well, it's done. And probably I am too." He stood up. "Would it be okay with you if we went along, Mrs. Gunning? I'd sort of like to get out of reach of the phone. Something tells me I'm going to get a phone call today and I'd like to put it off as long as possible."

"Now, Harry, that *is* stupid," Mrs. Gunning said. "The least you can do is call your father yourself, before he calls you." At Harry's expression she added, "That's my advice, but of course you'll have to do as you please."

In the station wagon, which he'd parked in front of the Gunnings', Harry gave Nan the package, no better wrapped than her mother's had been but more of a surprise. "For me?" she said.

"Who else? I just gave it to you, didn't I?"

"I was demurring."

"You aren't old enough to demur. That's for ladies who have something to demur about."

"Well, anyhow, it's awfully sweet of you."

"That's okay, Nan." His reply was nervous and distracted. "Look, don't open it yet." He put the car in gear, started slowly toward his own house, which was closer to the water and set apart on a large plot of land.

33

They went up the curving driveway, drew to a stop before Harry spoke again. "I'll make this phone call and then you can open it. The package."

"Want me to come in with you?"

"No! I mean, just stay here. I shouldn't be longer than all day." He leaped from the car and ran in the front door as though pursued. Mrs. Warner was there to meet him.

"Anything wrong, Aggie?" he asked.

"Why should something be wrong?"

"I don't know. Just seems like a good morning for it."

"It does at that," she said dryly, folding her heavy arms. "Getting nervous, Harry?"

"That doesn't begin to say what I'm getting. Mrs. Gunning says I should phone first. Before Dad does, I mean."

"That might be a finger in the dyke."

"You're a cheerful character," he said irritably. "I thought you'd—" He broke off.

"That I'd what?"

"Well, for Pete's sake, Aggie. Back me up. Or anyway say a word of comfort. Here I risk everything to get back to you, and what do I get? Breakfast and cold words."

"And ten dollars."

"Aggie—you phone for me." Mrs. Warner hesitated, shook her head. "Come on," he pressed. "It'd be easier for you than for me. At least sound him out for me."

"That would make things worse. Besides, you're

going to have to start facing the consequences of your own deeds, Harry."

He laughed. "I've never had a deed before. How could I face the consequences?"

"You know what I mean. You try to get other people to get between you and him. And, heaven knows, I've done it. I guess I wasn't doing you a favor that way, Harry."

"Fine time to start building my character, when I'm in trouble."

"Maybe a good time."

"You won't do it?"

Again she shook her head. Harry rubbed his neck, grabbed at the phone. "Then I'd better get at it fast." But his father, when he reached him at the apartment, was completely bewildered. "Harry?" he said. "What are you doing? What are you phoning me for?"

"To tell you why I'm here, Dad."

"Here? Where? Aren't you in your room? I mean, where *are* you?"

Harry swallowed. "At the Point, Dad."

There was a long silence. Harry began to think his father had gone to the bedroom to check. At length Mr. Lynch said, "Are you serious?"

"Well . . . yes, Dad."

"I see. Is there any explanation for this . . . astonishing behavior?"

"Not really, I guess. I'm sorry. Sorry if it bothers you, I mean, but—"

"Bothers me? That my son is not only disobedient but a sneak?"

"Dad . . . please. I'm not. Not really. I only . . . had to get out here, don't you see? I didn't see anybody when I was in there. You didn't even know I was gone, and you never seemed to listen when I—"

"I listened enough to say No, as I recall."

"Yes," Harry said.

"Harry, are you there?"

"Yes, sir."

"I don't know what to say to you. I'll have to think this over. In the meantime I presume you aren't going to leave the Point. No other place has struck your fancy? You aren't considering Spain or California?"

"No, sir." Why was it easier when his father became sarcastic? He's right and I'm wrong, Harry thought, but when he talks like that I don't mind so much. When he'd hung up, he turned to Mrs. Warner.

"Well?" she said.

"I don't know. He says he's going to think it over. Anyhow it's finished."

"You mean the phone call is finished."

"Did you know Warner's brother in the Bronx is sick?"

"Warner called me. You're avoiding the question."

"There's nothing to do but avoid it—till Friday." Suddenly he smiled at her. "I'm awfully glad to be here."

Mrs. Warner put her hand lightly on his arm. "I'm glad to have you. For the life of me," she muttered as though he were not supposed to hear, "I can't see why you'd have to stay down there either. Lot of nonsense."

"Well," Harry said briskly. "I'm off to pay my debtors with my borrowings." He waved and ran out the door. This was only Thursday and early in the morning. Friday could take care of itself.

Nan didn't open the present until after the trip to the post office. "I'm saving it," she explained. "Mother will make me a cake for lunch, and you'll be invited, and then I'll open it."

They played two sets of singles, swam, and then Harry lay down in the shade of a rock and fell asleep. When he awoke, Nan had the book open. She didn't notice him, so he had a moment to watch her, to see her as she would be when alone with something she loved. She ran the fingers of one hand up and down the binding of the book, and her eyes went carefully, with slow devotion, over every part of the plate she studied. There was wonder in her face and a special kind of solemnity. That Nan loved drawing and painting was obvious to anyone who knew her, but she had a lighthearted, impulsive attitude about her own work. She kept at it, yet with an air of amusement, as though she might at any moment toss it all aside. He hadn't understood till now how profoundly she'd learned to love the masters of the art she played at. I wonder how many people, he thought, of whom we never catch a glimpse in solitude, as I have Nan, remain to us always unknown. Nearly everyone, perhaps. It gave him a melancholy feeling.

"I thought you weren't going to open it," he said, sitting up.

Nan glanced over vaguely. "I wasn't. But I did."

She stared at the sea with wondering, remote eyes. "It's no wonder people want to go to Italy. All these beautiful things . . ." She sighed and turned back to him with a smile. "I suppose there should be some proper words of thanks, but I can't think of them."

"I'm thanked," he said simply.

"Harry, my boy," said a voice overhead. "And Miss Gunning. May I join this rendyvooze?" They looked up to see Philip Bowles ogling them from the top of the rock.

"The apeman cometh," muttered Nan as Philip scrambled down the rocks. "Open your hands," she said to him.

Philip kept his hands behind his back. "Now why, I ask? Why this peculiar command in place of a greeting?"

"I want to be sure there are no rubber tarantulas accidentally stuck in your fingers."

"Are you still bitter about that tarantula? I threw it at you because I thought it would make an interesting composition. 'Tarantula in Transition,' I'd titled it tentatively. I seem to have a T stuck in my teeth, but that's *all*." He brought his hands around swiftly in front of Nan's face, so that she jerked away, dropping her book in the sand.

"You imbecile," she said furiously. "Are you ever going to grow up?"

"I have no special plans at the moment, but when I do you can be sure you'll be the first to know."

"And the last to care."

"But you were the one who asked," Phil said. He

dropped beside them in the sand, indicated the book with his head. "What is this blot on the face of summer?" he asked, reaching for it.

Nan snatched it away. "I wouldn't let you so much as read the title."

Phil frowned. "Say, you really are steamed up today."

"I was perfectly all right until a few minutes ago."

"Maybe you're getting a summer cold. I hear they come on suddenly."

"Oh, I'm going home," Nan said. "Are you having lunch with us, Harry?"

"Sure," Harry said. "I'll go home and get dressed and be over as soon as I can make it."

"All right. Bye." As she walked away Phil looked after her speculatively. "Cute kid. But a disposition like ground glass."

Harry looked at him with disgust. "If you didn't act like the world's prime jackass every time you got near a girl, maybe you'd find their dispositions improved. Don't you ever bore yourself?"

"Not seriously."

Harry shrugged, and Phil went on, "No kidding, though. How do you get girls like Nan to like you?"

"Look, I've known Nan longer than I've known my father. And don't get her wrong, either. She's not interested, that way, in the genus male."

"Sort of retarded, wouldn't you say?"

"No, I wouldn't."

"She must be fifteen or sixteen."

"Sixteen. Just."

39

"Well, but I know girls of thirteen that stand my hair on end."

"Oh, you worldlings . . . what a devilish lot you are."

Phil, whose sense of humor had broad outlines, moved uncomfortably in the sarcastic element. "Cut it out, will you?" he said. He looked at Harry slyly. "What about you, Harry?"

"What do you mean, what about me?"

"The girls, boy, the girls."

Harry looked into Phil's unpleasantly shining eyes. "Save it for another time." He picked up his towel. "I'm not in the mood."

One of the most irritating things about Phil Bowles was that he didn't know how to take offense. That is, quite literally, he couldn't. No matter what you said, he took it. This had the maddening effect of making you speak more rudely than you meant to, which in turn made you angry with yourself and sorry for Phil. So then you had a try at toning down your words, whether to appease yourself or him made no difference, and wound up annoyed with everybody. Harry, beginning to feel the effects of lost sleep and the looming ordeal with his father, decided he'd be darned if he'd try any sort of palliation this time. Bowles could think what he wanted to.

"So long," he said, pulling on his T-shirt and getting determinedly to his feet. "See you around, Phil."

"Hey, wait a minute. I didn't ask you something.

What it is, I thought maybe next Saturday night—not this Saturday because I've got something else on—you could borrow the station wagon from your father and we could go over to Mills' Corners."

"Mills' Corners?" Harry echoed.

"Come off it, Harry. The place's okay," Phil said aggressively.

"I can't say, Phil. A week from Saturday's a long way off."

"Well, think it over, willya? We could really have a time."

"Can't you use your family's car?"

"Not on weekends anymore. I had it out last Friday when my father came down and he had to take a taxi. He didn't like it," Phil added reflectively.

They grinned at each other with sudden understanding and separated. But it's a peculiar thing, Harry thought, walking slowly toward his house, how if you act like Phil—horseplay and inanities and a conversation sieved of meaning—then people think you're a healthy lad. "A spirited, normal boy," Mr. Lynch was apt to say when he encountered Phil clowning for a group. "Why can't you be a little more like that, Harry? Not that I undervalue music and books, but all work and no play, you know . . ." And he'd waggle a lawyerish finger. "I'm not working when I listen to music," Harry would say unhopefully, and his father would invariably add something to the effect that carefree youth should not cloister itself in libraries and concert halls.

And as for *carefree,* Harry emphasized to himself, I couldn't be more restricted, more watched from a subtle distance, if I were heir apparent to the British throne. He remembered a time during his early school days when he had shouted in a tearful rage, "Warner must not come calling for me at school anymore. Everybody *laughs.* Nobody has people coming calling for them the way I do." His mother had looked at him—that loving, brooding gaze he recalled so clearly—for a long time before she said, "But it's been because I don't want you hurt, Harry. Because I love you." "If you do then you'll make him stop. They're *laughing* at me," he'd repeated hysterically. His mother, mercifully, had guessed how that laughter hurt, and he had been allowed to come from and go to school unescorted. But never ten minutes late. Even five minutes and he was sure to meet his mother or Warner or Aggie coming part way to meet him, to find out what was the matter . . . their expressions as they saw him being full of exaggerated relief. (Well, that wasn't strictly true. His mother's face had been like that. Aggie and Warner had always seemed satisfied but not unduly so.) In later years, of course, the watchfulness hadn't been so obvious.

Then during his mother's long illness he'd tried so hard to spare her anxiety—she worried whenever he or Margaret was out—that he'd wound up practically friendless. No, sorry, he could not join the Latin Club, it took too much time after school. Nor the Drama Club. No, too bad, but in spite of being tall and clearly in good health, he could not be on the basketball team

42

or the soccer team. People began to think he was odd, and no wonder. Balanced against that had been the look on his mother's face when he came into the big, airy front bedroom, and she turned as she lay on the chaise before the window to say, "Oh, Harry—how nice to see you." He and his mother had been able to talk to each other for hours. Margaret, who also tried her best to stay within reach, could never understand that. "I just don't know what to say after a while," she'd tell Harry unhappily. "I get sad. And nervous." "It's all right," Harry would tell her. "I'm around, and she can talk to me. You go along over to Anne's, and I'll tell Mom you'll be back later."

But since his mother had died, the supervision, under his father's direction, had taken on the aspect of surveillance. Go where you will, he seemed to say, my eyes are always upon you.

"Who does he think he is, anyhow?" Harry demanded now, slamming in the back door.

"Your father?" Aggie said, not pretending to misunderstand.

"Yeah. It isn't as if he really cared a darn about me."

"Stop that, Harry. He does, and you know it. Have you ever stopped to wonder what it would be like to be a man trying to bring up two children, not really knowing how to because you'd never done it? Your father's doing the best he knows how to guide you and Margaret."

"We aren't children. And this isn't guidance, it's thralldom."

"Harry, I have no patience with you when you talk this way. Are you eating here?"

"No, at the Gunnings'. They're having a birthday cake for Nan."

"Well, why don't you spruce up a bit."

"That's what I intended to do, Aggie," he said pointedly. "Can't anyone ever let me do anything without telling me first of all that I should? Don't you think I could work that out myself . . . lunch, party, clean clothes?" He stamped off angrily, shouting, "Leave me alone!"

Aggie Warner looked after him, shaking her head. Since he'd been a little boy, Harry, when nervous or alarmed, had taken refuge in rudeness. It was not an attractive quality but seemed to be lessening. Mr. Lynch would argue, as she did herself often enough, that to let such moments pass unrebuked was not to Harry's best interest. But I don't know, she thought now. It seemed as if one way or the other Harry's best interest was too much served. Nagged at and corrected and watched over like a boy half his age. ("Well," Mr. Lynch would say, "if he acts half his age, he'll have to be treated as such.") Harry tried to shift his responsibilities—as this morning he had tried to put the phone call off on her—he was careless with money; he lost and forgot things and sulked sometimes like a ten-year-old. Mr. Lynch seemed to feel that everything wrong was Harry's fault and everything good the direct reflection of excellent upbringing. Well, Harry was responsible, so were all the rest of them, for the good and the bad, and that was what Mr. Lynch would

44

not admit. Warner and I, now, she thought. We protect him one time, tell him to stand on his feet the next, but never with any pattern, any consistency. And yet this morning he was pretty good about that phone call. He didn't want to make it and tried to get out of it, but when he had to, he did it. Was that Harry? Or his upbringing? Mr. Lynch, with his nervous desire not to be disturbed, had often allowed Harry to do ridiculous things just to get him out of the way. And Mrs. Lynch herself, who had loved Harry more than anyone else in the world, had, when she was ill and wanting him, not been brave enough to deny herself.

It's a wonder, Mrs. Warner thought now, getting out the vacuum, carrying it into the living room, that he's managed to get as far as he has on this road to the grown-up state. Having made the trip herself, she did not envy Harry all its aspects.

Harry went out the back door, through the hedge, and across the road on his way to the Gunnings'. There were no sidewalks here. You just walked in the grass or at the edge of the road itself, beside the hedges, the fences, the open lawns. About half a mile, most of it under old trees that met in bridges overhead. The sun through the leaves fell like a gold fishnet, and now and then a bird complained about noontime. A dog barked, and a baby cried, and a lawn mower whirred, stopped, and whirred again. There was Sam Morely, who went to school with Harry, trimming privet. He sheared a leaf from the bush, stepped back to get the effect, advanced upon another leaf.

"Hi, Harry," he said.

"Hi, Sam."

At every house, flung on clotheslines or over back porch railings, were bathing suits and sandy-looking towels, rubber caps hanging by their chinstraps. There in the Jaffes' yard was the baby sitting in his playpen, staring with meticulous care at a caterpillar that humped across the floor of his little world. With a sudden dart of his chubby hand he seized the caterpillar and crammed it into his mouth. Harry turned his head away and walked faster. Someone had told him that babies did things like that. He'd never believed it before. Not very tasty, I guess. But not lethal. So anyway the Jaffe baby will survive that. He thought about all the things to be survived which still lay before the Jaffe baby, before himself, before Aggie and his father. Only his mother was delivered. But, oh, for her not to be alive on a day like this . . . the sort of day she loved —sun-steeped and indolent, like a yellow butterfly opening and closing its wings. Pain tightened in him, but he could bear it now. In the beginning he'd thought he wouldn't be able to, when it came clawing at him with its terrible strength and there was nowhere to hide. And he'd been cold all the time. He couldn't get his fingers warm, and at night he'd lie under the blankets shivering. Nowhere, nowhere . . . He would dream that he'd come in after school, and there she'd be, sitting on a chair arm, swinging a slim leg, grinning at him. "Have a good day?" she'd ask. And through the almost intolerable joy he'd say, "But I thought you were dead, I thought that you had died." "Ah, Harry," she'd say softly, "Ah, love . . . You see, it isn't true." *Come back, come back,* he'd cry when he woke. And never, never, the silence would tell him. Yet now as he walked along this road she had walked, the pain within him was a thing he could carry. He thought how often she would have passed this very spot, here beside the amber beech he stopped to lean against, and listened to the very sounds that he heard now. The rustle overhead as a bird flicked through leaves, the music of the incoming tide booming on the reefs, on the rocks. The cry of gulls, the sweet wooden tone of a cowbell in the field beyond. He tried to listen for them both—for his mother, for himself.

Mrs. Gunning yawned, pushed her plate aside and surveyed the two alert young people. Exhausting, she thought, and glanced around the littered kitchen, wondering how far observance of Nan's birthday would have to carry her. Up with the roosters. Popovers, cake, and now all these dirty dishes. They were such sweet children, so endlessly supplied with power. I wish they'd go away for a while, she thought, so I could lie down. Only I wish they'd do the dishes first.

"One more week," she said, "and then your father's vacation begins."

"That'll be nice," Nan said, adding with a smile,

47

"even worth having the radio on all day."

"Oh, the radio," Mrs. Gunning said vaguely. "I just ignore it."

"I can't," Nan said. "Especially the ads. The minute one of those creamy voices begins begging me to buy something, I have to drop everything I'm doing and listen. It's a sort of compulsion."

"Interesting," Harry said. "It probably means you're short on will power."

"Anyone who gets up at six-thirty of her own volition isn't short on will power," Mrs. Gunning said firmly.

"Why does he play the radio all the time?" Harry asked.

Nan and Mrs. Gunning shook their heads. "He says he likes a background," Nan recalled.

Harry had to smile. The minute Mr. Gunning arrived that radio was put on, quite low, and except, Harry supposed, for sleeping hours it never went off till he left. Funny about life, Harry thought. In you come with no tastes or preferences at all, and then in a little while there you are loving what others ignore, disliking or perhaps never even finding something they dote upon. He wondered what, for instance, the Jaffe baby would come to love—once he'd gotten over his taste for insects, of course. Was he, sitting there in his playpen on a sunny morning, growing imperceptibly toward a great devotion to . . . baseball, maybe? Like Phil Bowles's little brother, who never thought of anything else? In twenty years it was conceivable that that fuzz-munching baby would stuff a wad of tobacco in

48

his cheek, lean over and test the ashwood bats, heft one to his liking, and take a stance that would send shivers of delight or despair down the best part of the nation's spines. Or perhaps a baton in place of a bat? Thirty, forty years, and Maestro Jaffe, in rehearsal with the Boston Symphony . . . beautiful hands drawing, describing . . . kindly (imperious?) voice lauding, chiding . . . *Horns, ah, lovely, lovely. Celli! No, no, no, celli! You cannot do that, that is not allowed. Don't you think Brahms knew his instruments? Lift, lift the bows . . . so . . .* Or possibly he'd grow to nothing great. To the simple wonderful pleasure of being in the bleachers, in the balcony, spellbound with his fellows by the batter, the conductor. But feeling, caring.

"Richard London's coming down to spend his entire vacation with us," he said abruptly.

"Richard London," Nan said. "It always sounds made up. Did you hear about the two flies that landed on Robinson Crusoe?" Mrs. Gunning and Harry shook their heads. "Well, one decided to fly away and the other one said, 'So long, I'll see you on Friday.'" She looked at two carefully unsmiling faces. "Just happened to think of it. Pity you feel you can't laugh."

Mrs. Gunning did, but Harry said unforgivingly, "That's adolescent."

"Me too," Nan said placidly. "Harry, let's do the dishes so Mom can get upstairs before she falls asleep."

"If you really feel you must," Mrs. Gunning said. She rose. "Any normal person would be exhausted in this house, with you and Harry bounding around like anodes and cathodes—if that's what I'm thinking of.

49

. . ." Her voice trailed away as she left the kitchen.

"Mother's cute," Nan said. She looked at Harry for confirmation, and her face was suddenly filled with concern. "Does that bother you, Harry?"

"Talking about your mother?" He picked up a dish towel, shook his head. "No. Don't think things like that, Nan. It would make a sort of difference. I don't want any differences."

"What do you want, Harry? Is that a silly question?"

He smiled. "Maybe. I don't know what I want. Do you?"

"Nothing. Not now, anyway. I have everything I want. Harry, I do adore the book. I'll cherish it all my life."

"All your life. You certainly make reckless statements."

"No. No, Harry. There are some things I'm sure of. Things I know."

Chapter 3

Henry lynch, upright, methodical, rather shy, had often wished he'd remained a bachelor. When he first met Katherine, her airy indifference to system and rules had filled him with delighted horror. In a sort of enchantment he married her, and within that enchantment had continued to love her. But living with her had proved an affliction. Would *nothing* ever run smoothly? Would they always be late to engagements, involved with embarrassing nonconformists, left with this sense of loose ends flapping about like fringe? Would she never never cease dashing in at the last minute, or later, with that "Darling, are you absolutely furious with me? I *know* I promised to get here earlier, but . . ." Would she never get over that absurd love for the house on the Point? "Henry, we *can't* accept the judge's invitation. I promised the kids a picnic on the sand at night. . . . Oh, you'll love it. . . ." Knowing perfectly well that he wouldn't love it. It had been part of her stubborn attempt to bring him into closer contact with the children. Why in the world, he had wondered often and irritably, does this ridiculous American picture of the jolly Pop obtain? Did every man in the country except himself *want* to play Bears, to make an ass of himself essaying sports intended for young bones and spirits, or even, for that matter, to take his offspring to marionette shows on Saturday afternoons? "I don't want to be a pal, dammit!" he'd yelled one day. "I want to bring my children up in dignity and comfort to be creditable citizens, and that's all!"

"Don't use that revolting word," Katherine had said mildly.

"Pal?" He'd said it to annoy her and was glad he had.

"Creditable."

Henry Lynch drew a quick breath. "Katherine—" he said, but did not know how to go on.

And then Katherine had fallen ill and a dark knowledge hung above them all for months. After the first panic Henry had had a furtive, constantly fought-down and constantly renewed sense of relief at the way his life was running. Mrs. Warner took over the direction of the house, he arrived at his engagements punctually, his home was no longer cluttered with odd people talking about things he didn't understand, and his children were clearly willing to conduct their social affairs without his assistance. His heart was breaking, but his life, it seemed, was smoothing out in spite of that. And Katherine died so almost peacefully. He sometimes thought that he had never loved her more than during those months when he would spend hours in the bedroom, reading to her, talking quietly.

And yet that evening had come. . . . "You seem so calm," he'd said, lulled by an hour of Emerson, by the claret sunset flowing over Central Park, by Katherine's face, still and reposeful against pale-blue pillows. "So calm and so beautiful."

She turned to him slowly and for a long time looked into his eyes without speaking. "Calm?" she said at length.

Henry, with a fearful revelation at length before him, had leaned forward and put his face on the blankets. Calm, calm . . . that was what he wanted, that was what he'd have. Soon now all the ordered calm that even he could wish. Even this morning he'd been thinking vaguely, without putting dates to it, that perhaps Harry would like a prep school away from home when . . . He shuddered, putting out his hand to clutch his wife's. He whispered, "Katherine, what are we going to do?"

"Don't you think I've wondered? Don't you think I've lain here, wondering, and . . . How much courage do you think I have, Henry, that you tell me I'm so calm and beautiful?"

"All the courage, all the courage," he said painfully, turning his head. He could not look up.

She put her other hand on his hair. It might have looked like benediction or forgiveness, but he felt the tension, the tremor, the rein. It was the hand of a woman wanting to hold hard, knowing she could not. "None at all," she said. "Do you understand, Henry? None at all. Only some pride, and love." And Katherine, who wept lightly and easily, was crying with bitter restraint. It was a sound of wreckage and ruin there in the luxurious room, a sound of rout and fear. *My God, my God, why hast Thou forsaken us?* The most terrible, the never answered, question.

After she died he devoted himself, in the way he could, to his children. Made sure they understood how important they were to him. (And did they remember how often he'd overlooked them in the past? No doubt, but you can only proceed from the present, do what you can.) He never suggested that Harry go away to school. He kept the house at the Point, though it was a nuisance and a liability. He kept close watch on their comings and goings, though without, he thought, too much restriction. He even tried to edge Mrs. Warner out of their affairs so as to occupy a larger place himself, but when it appeared that Mrs. Warner would either edge out completely or not at all, he had to abandon that. As the months passed, his life assumed almost the status he had longed for. Orderly, disciplined. The office, the club. All very unenterprising, very satisfying. The single flaw was

Harry. And what, Mr. Lynch wondered, was the method of procedure there? The boy had always seemed, in past years, tractable enough. Oh, a childish rebellion here and there no doubt, but those had been handled by Katherine or Mrs. Warner and had been dissipated or forgotten. This was different. Katherine's death had changed them all, but chiefly Harry. For himself, after the first deep grief a pensive sadness, in its way not unpleasant, had settled upon him. Katherine was with him always, in a closer, quieter way than she had ever been with him alive. And Margaret . . . Well, Margaret. He recognized in his daughter a quality of his own—a reluctance, a positive inability to support large emotions. Love, grief, even happiness. It must be like the differing tolerances for drugs, he thought. Some can absorb great quantities. Some, like Margaret and himself, only moderate doses. He did not regret his incapacity. Margaret's illness and desolation at her mother's death had been pitiful to watch, and he'd breathed a sigh of relief when at length her natural limitations had brought them to a slow climax and end. The lift of her head when he mentioned a new young law clerk in the office, a dress he'd noticed in Bergdorf's window, a play for which it was almost impossible to get tickets but there was just a chance . . . All the returning signs of self-interest. Of course Margaret still loved and missed her mother, but life, he told himself, is for the living, and he welcomed the arrival of Richard London despite the fact that Richard seemed to Henry a bit bland.

But Harry— Well, circle and avoid as he might, he had to get back to Harry. In the beginning, in what Henry considered a most unnatural, most unfilial manner, Harry had refused to mention his mother at all. (But Harry had gone to the funeral when Margaret had had to be put to bed.) He'd get up and go out of a room if Margaret or her father made any reference to Katherine. Henry, confused and anguished, had not protested the incivility, though he thought now he should have. Probably he should have done a great many things he'd omitted to do, but even with hindsight he couldn't quite see what they were. Harry had become a difficult, recessive, unreasonable person, and all his father's attempts to establish closeness through affectionate guidance had come to nothing. And now this business of running away. Granted that Harry seemed to care about only one thing, that house at the Point; granted he'd been a little restless this week in the city (and that, Henry told himself with a trace of righteousness, was planned only for their benefit, Margaret's and Harry's); granted that unfortunately the return had been delayed, necessitating Harry's being left somewhat alone. Granted all these —very minor—circumstances: None of them justified a flagrant piece of disobedience that would have to be punished, heaven knew how.

Henry Lynch sat at his desk, rubbing his chin between thumb and forefinger, and dealt with vexation upon the importance of punishing Harry. It is time, he told himself, to take a firm stand. Spare the rod and—well, Harry was scarcely a child anymore, but a boy of seventeen could not be allowed to flout authority. The juvenile courts were filled every day with children and young people who never knew how far they could go unchecked. Who were, perhaps, in trouble from trying to find out. Harry would have to be punished, kindly but sternly. Henry sighed and looked at a triple-framed picture beside the inkwell. Katherine, in a snapshot, turning unsuspectingly toward the camera, pushing her bright hair back with a quizzical expression. It was a glimpse of her he'd caught one day in the garden at the Point. He'd been snapping the rosebushes, so magnificently in bloom, and Katherine had come around the arbor, deep in thought. "Katherine," he'd called softly, and she had turned with that odd inquiring look. So now he had her forever at that moment on his desk. He sometimes wondered what she'd been thinking about. There was a cabinet portrait of Margaret, reduced to fit the frame. A seraphic prettiness and not much else, but that was typical of the photographer who'd done it. A snapshot of Harry, also taken at the Point. He was squinting a little, not at the camera but toward the sea. He wore tennis clothes and his build was magnificent. Henry had wondered before where Harry might have gotten this powerful physique in a family of rather wanly delicate proportions on both sides. Margaret had taken this picture last summer, when Katherine's illness had been first suspected. Henry picked up the frame and studied his son's face closely. Of course you couldn't tell much from a snapshot. Still, was there in those dark narrowed eyes, that handsome

tempting to disguise from himself the fact that the proposed punishment was merely a salve, and not a very good one, to his own conscience—that's another thing. Do normal, spirited teen-agers spend that much time listening to music? Why can't he be more like Sam or Phil or those other boys. Why out of all those boys at the Point should mine be the *different* one? It was all so disorderly. There was no harmony in life lately, none at all. He only wanted peace. Was that too much to ask? Of course it's too much to ask, said an echo in his mind, but he refused to listen. Peace, though distractingly difficult of attainment under certain circumstances, was not too much to ask.

The intercom buzzed, and his secretary informed him that Miss Lynch and Warner were on their way for him in the car. "Thank you, Mrs. Farmer." He straightened his desk, made a phone call, and prepared to leave just as Margaret came into the office.

"Was there something you wanted?" he asked, picking up his briefcase and going to the closet for his straw hat. "We'd better get downstairs. Warner can't park outside the building indefinitely."

"Why did you think I wanted something?" she asked, and added at her father's impatient expression, "Oh, well, yes. I do. The thing is, Dad . . . I wondered if we could pick Richard up."

"Pick him up? When?"

"Well, *now*, on our way out. I think it would be nice to drive him out with us." She eyed him hopefully. Her father loathed being in the car for any time with strangers. He considered strangers all those people not his colleagues, or in his family, or whom he had not known for twenty years. He was courteous and almost benign toward Richard when the two met, but that was always under circumstances which almost immediately took them apart. The drive to the Point by car took a good two hours. Maybe some girls could wind their fathers around their little fingers, Margaret thought wistfully, but hers was definitely unwindable. Probably she should have let Richard take the train and been glad to have him at all. Of course, since her father was only at the Point on weekends, and sometimes missed those, Richard wouldn't really be much in his way. And she had to be fair; Dad had never refused to let them have their friends either out there or at the apartment. He only required that he be left alone, and that was preferable to the attitude of some parents she knew, who hung about like familiars and spoiled all the fun. She began to wish she hadn't suggested driving Richard out with them. It would have been awfully nice and all, but—

"All right," Henry Lynch said. "But we'd better get going."

She needn't have looked so surprised, he told himself, settled in the car on the far side of Richard, on their way at last. Yet he had to admit stirrings of distaste for Richard London in such close proximity. The fellow talked all the time, occasionally addressing Henry despite the fact that Henry was trying to read his weekly news magazine. And Richard tapped. Tapped his foot, his fingers on the windowsill, his hand on his thigh. You couldn't ignore the fact that

Richard was in the car, couldn't ignore the drive itself, as Henry usually managed to. Contrast this with the drive down on Monday, which had been so peaceful, completed before you'd really given much thought to it. Henry scowled at his magazine.

"Bad news, sir?" said Richard, leaning around Margaret.

"What's that? Oh, of course there's bad news. The news is terrible all the time."

"Isn't it, though?" Richard said as though pleased that they'd found a point in common. "Now, take Kenya—" He stopped.

"Well? What about Kenya?"

"Man I know says the situation there is worsening again. They once had holdings there. This man, that is. His family."

Henry looked at him in horror for a moment, turned back to *Time* without a word. The fellow's nothing but a fool, he thought. A perfect ass. He hoped Margaret was not serious here, was only killing time. Stupefying would be a better term, he decided.

"I ran into Grace Revere the other day," Margaret was saying. "When I was having lunch with Dotty. She asked about you." There was a note of pique in her voice.

"Really?" said Richard.

"Well, I just thought I'd mention it. She looked about thirty. Richard?"

"Yes?"

"Did you know there are cracks in the Pan Am Building?"

"Margaret, darling, there can't be cracks in the Pan Am Building. You've been having optical illusions."

"Oh, no. Dotty saw them too. Under that sort of suspended piece, you know, on the ceiling. Big cracks."

"Well, I'll go over and look, but it seems darned funny. If there are cracks, it'll just be the surface plaster. Nothing serious."

"Still, it doesn't look right. For the architect, you know. Dotty wants to know if we'll go to the Paul Scofield with her and Peter."

"Good idea. Shall I get the tickets?"

"I don't know. Dotty didn't say. Maybe Peter's going to get them."

"Better find out. Tell them any time at all. That is, if any time suits you. We could even run in from the Point, couldn't we, if it came to that?"

"We could. But why don't we wait till we get back?"

"Fine with me." Richard tapped his cheek with one finger. "That's just the underside of the ceiling, you know. It has nothing to do with the structure at all."

"Huh? Oh, the Pan Am Building. Well, so long as you say so. Richard?"

"Yes, Margaret?"

"You remember that place you were telling me about, the one that makes the Oysters Rockefeller? Well . . ."

Mr. Lynch held his magazine tightly, reading and rereading the same paragraph.

The rocks stretched far out into the water, and there were times during storms when the waves rode over them in turbulent whitened walls, fell away, and came crashing back tremendously as though they would never have done with assaulting the land. Yet today that great beast, the ocean, was docile as a lion in heaven. Rather the color of a lion too. Clear but tawny under the sun. Low waves brushed against the gray rocks, curling and glinting, and above the water line split-shelled barnacles and amber seaweed and salt dried in the heat. The air was filled with a sea smell. Burning sand, beached fish, ocean, and silver marsh grass—it was all drawn together and sifted by the sun.

Early Friday afternoon. The beach was studded with brilliant umbrellas, towels, blankets, mounds of clothes secured by shoes, dark glasses, oily shoulders, brown bodies, tin shovels. The lazy surf flapped at the sand, poured away, rolled in again, and each time the face of the shore was altered. The waves came in, churned the sand, slid back to sea, leaving a lacy foam that winked and disappeared. The sand flattened, darkened. Little things burrowed. Then the next wave came in and it was all to do again, with altered patterns, new shells.

Nan reclined in the shallow water, kicking her legs, reluctant to get out. I won't remember that it's midsummer, she told herself. I'll forget that the noon of our time here has passed. The low waves came in and broke against her, over her.

Harry lay far out on the rocks, his chin on his hands,

watching a ruffle of smoke on the horizon. It wasn't much, just a puff trailing backward, and you couldn't see the ship, but it meant people were out there on the water, bound for somewhere; people he didn't know, would never know, whose existence for him was signified only by a little line of smoke and only because he'd been watching the sea at this particular moment. He sat up, trying to see the last feathers of the plume of smoke, but the air trembled in the sun's light, and the sea was so brilliant that he couldn't be sure what he saw.

He started back along the rocks, stopping now and then to watch a seagull ride the swells or lift with a sudden strength of wings at his approach and go crying away. "See . . . see . . . see . . ." the gulls cried as they hovered and hung and dived. Their voices mingled with the voices of people on the beach, with the lazy clapper of the buoy at the end of the rocks, with the shush of the water advancing, receding, Harry turned away from the beach, went across a small field, through a gate in the high boxwood hedge, around the arbor, down the walk, and so home. Whenever you came in now on a bright afternoon, the house was like this—cool and dim as a trout pool, ordered and silent. The big hall clock ticked away the minutes, the furniture in the shadowed living room looked apart, unused, the flowers in their porcelain bowls unreal. We should put plush ropes across the doors, Harry thought, going upstairs.

He took a shower, returned to his room, leaving

sand in the shower stall and his towel in a heap on the floor, got into jeans and a white short-sleeved shirt, and was ready to leave when Aggie knocked at the door.

"I wanted to be sure you'd come home," she said when he opened the door. "Your father will probably want to see you."

"Most probably," Harry agreed.

Mrs. Warner's glance strayed past him to the crumpled shorts and T-shirt flopping on the chair arm. Shaking her head, she went to pick them up, glanced into the bathroom, and nodded as though she'd found just what she expected to find.

"Something wrong, Aggie?" he asked and then, "Oh, blast. I forgot. Here, I'll clear up this stuff." He tried to take the clothes and wet towel from her, and when that proved useless, bent over and swished ineffectually at the sand in the shower stall. "Maybe if I just run the shower a bit, it'll wash down." He turned it on, jumped just in time to escape a drenching, reached in and turned it off, and regarded the result triumphantly. "There. All fixed."

Mrs. Warner studied him without speaking and once again shook her head.

"Well, what's wrong now?" he demanded. "This is a heck of a lot of fuss over a few grains of sand."

"It isn't the sand, Harry. How many times, how *many* times have I asked you not to drop things around as if an automatic slave were following you with nothing to do but straighten the trail?"

65

"Couple of dozen, I guess. I'm sorry. I keep forgetting." He grinned. "Oh, come on, Aggie. I don't mean to drop the darn things."

"I know you don't mean— Come on downstairs. You can help me with the silver if you like."

"Sure."

They went down side by side, along the carpeted quiet hall to the kitchen, where all the windows were open and the sun flooded in. On the table completed silver flashed in the light, but there was a depressing assortment, coated with gray-pink polish, on the sideboard. "Why are we doing all this?" Harry asked.

"Your sister is having a guest. We want things nice for her."

"Who's going to know whether this stuff is polished or not? Except you and me," he added glumly. "We'll know for sure."

"The thing about silver," Aggie told him, getting to work, "is that you don't notice if it is, but you do notice if it isn't. That's the thing about a lot of housework."

"I'm glad I'm not a woman."

"Well, so am I. We'd certainly have a job to marry you off."

"I'm not at all sure I'd allow myself to be married off. I think women usually get the short end of that stick. Housework and kids and some slob who thinks he's done you a favor."

"Is that your picture of marriage?"

"It's a picture. What do I know about it? Maybe women don't care about freedom."

"And what would you say freedom was?"

"Godalmighty, Aggie, what's freedom to anybody? Being able to do what you want."

Oh, a long way to go, Aggie thought. Such a long way.

". . . and besides, she missed the entire point of the conversation, as far as I'm concerned," Margaret was saying to Richard. "All that nonsense about did they or didn't they like French Provincial. She was being *offered* blond mahogany and lucky to get it, too. After all, they paid for the entire honeymoon—her parents I mean—which simply isn't done, and on top of that to fuss about the furnishings. Well, all I can say is, neither of them has showed a scrap of taste from start to finish. Richard, this isn't a very nice thing to say, but don't you get the feeling that maybe he . . . you know . . ."

"You mean her parents' money?" Richard supplied. He shrugged slightly. "How would anyone ever know? Really know? If they manage to put a good face on it—"

Henry Lynch stared through his window with trapped desperation. Short of screaming or ordering the idiot out of his car, there was nothing at all to do about this. Two hours, two solid hours, of the most utter tripe he'd ever heard uttered in or out of a courtroom had left him with a weak sort of longing to see Harry. Harry could be about as exasperating as any human Henry had ever encountered, but he did not talk tripe. Is this really Margaret? he wondered. I do

67

not believe it. I don't believe this twaddling foolish girl is my daughter. She's been duped. Here is Titania beside me, and there's her long-eared jackass, Bottom, who's to spend his entire vacation with us. Gratefully he saw Piff's Junction in the distance. Twenty minutes and they'd be home. He hadn't thought of Piff's Prance as home in a long time. In his mind they always went "out there" and then came home to the apartment, but today the solid, still reality of his study (and let Mr. London try to get in there) was home, the waiting empty presence of his bedroom was home. He wondered why he hadn't ridden with Warner. It was too late now to change, but by heaven if he ever got in such a situation again, either he'd ride with Warner or the guests would ride in the trunk.

And still he hadn't thought of what to say to Harry. It wasn't possible to think, cooped up with these chatterboxes. Cut his allowance in half, Henry repeated to himself for the dozenth time. But what to say? What was he going to say? Again he was tempted to say nothing, to ignore the whole business. And again pride, the voice of authority, intervened. Harry, I am doing this for your own good. No, it was clearly impossible to speak those words. True, of course, but rendered by usage useless. They had almost comic overtones. This is going to hurt you more than it does me, and so forth. We have dug the grave of many a truth with our tongues, he thought. Those that are left had better look to their safety. From the trifling matter of chastising a son to the fateful business of conducting human affairs, nowhere was truth your outspoken ally any longer; nowhere did you find her naked and unashamed. In order to survive in our times, he thought, truth needs a lot of concealing garments. By the day we have done with piling on the disguising layers, we may never even notice if she's disappeared altogether. He sighed and realized that once again he'd wandered. It was always this way when he tried to think about his children. He began with great purpose and ended grazing among his own thoughts, which were usually general, rarely personal. But now —about Harry.

". . . and I don't know," Margaret was saying, "I just don't like the movies anymore. This may sound silly, but I feel the way the kids do—too much smooching goes on in the movies. I like to see somebody fighting mountain lions, something like that. But all these couples sitting in each other's laps . . . it gets boring."

"Neatest trick of the week." Richard chuckled. "No, but I see what you mean. Trouble is, you've been going to the wrong kind. You go to these good foreign films and then complain because there aren't any mountain lions. Now, take Westerns—"

"Will you shut up!" Henry snapped, as much to his own surprise as to theirs.

"Dad, please," Margaret said, putting her hand toward Richard, who took it wordlessly.

At least something can make him wordless, Henry thought, muttering an apology. He folded his arms and sank back with a slight feeling of triumph. The drive was completed in silence, but once at the house the air was fretted with voices. Aggie came out to greet them with a robust welcome that Henry found overdone.

"Well, Mr. Lynch," she said loudly, "you're looking very fit, very fit indeed. And Margaret . . . my goodness, isn't that a new dress? What have you been doing with yourself in the gay town all week? How are you, Mr. London? I hope you'll enjoy your stay with us. I have your room all ready for you, so if Warner will just take the bags . . ." She herded them about, like a shepherd blowing on a tuba, Henry told himself, and the only normal remark he heard her make was a soft, "How are you, dear? How's Jack now?" to her husband. The mother bird, Henry decided. Squawking and dragging her wings to distract the enemy from her fledgling. Well, he thought, might as well get it over with. Displeased, still undecided, but resolute, he said, "Ask Harry to come in and see me, will you, Mrs. Warner," and fled the scene of bags and greetings.

He was leaning against the study desk—strange how desks reassured him—looking rather absently at the garden when Harry came in. "Hello, son," he said. "The roses . . ." He turned and saw Harry's unyielding face and was jerked back to the task in hand. Indeed he had only forgotten it during the fleetest second of looking at the roses. "Sit down, please. We are going to have a talk."

Talk, my foot, Harry thought. We are going to

mete out justice. He sat down, waiting. For a while his father said nothing and they did not look at each other.

"An engineer," Mr. Lynch began at last, relieved that he had finally hit upon a thing to say, "is commissioned to build a bridge." He allowed a pause, during which they would both establish the fact that this was an analogy, that the hearing would be unemotional. "I think you will agree that nothing but stupidity or criminal negligence will induce him to try to span a river with poor materials, arguing that he will go back and strengthen the weak places later." Another pause. "You will agree to that?" Harry nodded, and despite his resolve, Mr. Lynch began to feel vexed. "I think a more courteous reply is called for, Harry," he said sharply.

"Yes, sir," said Harry with no expression.

Not mollified, Henry continued. "Our engineer, if he is an honest man and has at heart the best interests of the . . . ah . . . the people—" (He was beginning to see that his analogy was not well chosen and might even prove unwieldy if Harry decided to point out that the mythical engineer hadn't gotten around to the hypothetical bridge until it was practically completed.) "Our engineer must see to it that his bridge is soundly built from the very beginn—all the way. Now, if the engineer should, in the course of construction, encounter a dangerously weak spot . . ."

Harry half listened, wondering how long it would go on. Another man than his father would probably

71

abandon bridge and builder here and get down to cases. But his father was a lawyer first, and even though his case was weak would undoubtedly try to bull it through, relying on the denseness of the jury to obscure the flaws. Except, thought Harry, I'm not the jury. I'm the fellow in the dock, and here's the judge, jury, and attorneys for both sides all rolled up in one. He considered demolishing the bridge motif, or at least pointing out a few "dangerously weak spots" that his father was undoubtedly aware of anyway, but there didn't seem to be much use. He'd only prolong things and exasperate his father further (that was a good pair of words) and make the finale harsher than it need be. He had a feeling his father's heart wasn't really in this. Besides, he was himself quite ready to admit that in his father's eyes he had done something very wrong. But his father had called it "disobedience." The humiliating childishness of the term hardened and angered him, and he was sure that the sentence imposed would be one suited to a child. Why can't he *look* at me? Why can't he see what anyone else could, that I'm not a child, that I'm a person with rights? Why couldn't they talk, as his father had implied they would, but as they never, of course, did?

"We must strengthen you, Harry, as we go along." Henry Lynch exhaled a long breath. Summations ended, charge read, jury will now find as it has been told to find. "My decision is to cut your allowance in half."

Harry was more ashamed even than he'd expected

72

to be. Why didn't he simply have me put to bed without my supper? Or I might have stood in a corner. Why didn't he think of that? A sudden panic shivered through him. They never were going to let him grow up. He was going to be one of those pathetic asses who go to college or land in the army and just can't take it because they've been so coddled and directed that they're incapable of making a decision, unable to tolerate any discipline higher than the nursery level, unable to stand at all without a dozen adolescent crutches for support. He'd heard of fellows like that, who slunk back to go to nearby schools and live at home, who in spite of youth and health got thrown out of the services. They came back, some ashamed, some defiant, some simply relieved, but all *stamped*. Abruptly he was standing. "May I go now?" Not waiting for an answer, he left the room.

Henry Lynch, unspeakably depressed, watched him go. It was all so difficult. Difficult and confusing and exhausting. He hadn't supposed that Harry would mind so much having his allowance cut. It had seemed, in point of fact, a rather mild and reasonable punishment. I just don't understand them, he told himself. I don't understand Margaret and that knuckle-headed architect. I don't understand Mrs. Warner and her attitude of censure. I don't understand *Harry*.

He shook his head and looked frowning toward the garden. It was impossible to recapture that moment of reverie induced by the roses just a little while ago.

* * *

"I was reading somewhere or other," Richard London said at dinner, "that in many cases when they open these Egyptian sarcophaguses—sarcophagi?—the mummy just poofs to dust, like that"—he snapped his fingers—"the minute the air hits it."

"That's what's going to happen to Grace Revere," Margaret said, "if she ever takes her makeup off in the daylight."

Richard smiled. "No, but it's really very interesting. Some of these archaeologists say that the Egyptians, far from being such expert embalmers, actually spoiled the mummies with all their spices and fluids. Bodies just buried in the sand survived better. It's the dry climate, it seems, that preserved them so beautifully. Thanks," he said to Warner, who stood beside him with a platter of asparagus. He helped himself and said, "I certainly will," to an offer of hollandaise. "It's a perfect sauce. I've found that hollandaise, which only requires a little care in preparation, is nearly always ruined, even in good restaurants, by the mistake of using too much lemon. This one's wonderful, though." He began to eat with a relish that proved his words were no exaggeration.

His words are not anything, Harry thought. They signify less than the sound of a few pebbles falling off a wall because something has brushed past them.

Henry looked at his daughter and thought, Can she actually be fond of a man who discusses embalming fluid in the same breath with hollandaise? Apparently she could. She talked with her Richard cheerfully, following the will-o'-the-wisp of his mind and follow-ing, Henry noted, with great adroitness. Like a pair of flies they buzzed about aimlessly, lit here, lit there, shot away, returned. He glanced at his son and smiled a little. Harry was studying Richard with the thought-ful regard of a man not only deciding not to buy but wondering how the article had been put up for sale to begin with. Harry shifted his glance and met his father's. Their amusement mingled in a moment of unusual closeness before they looked away.

But, Harry thought, I won't let that disarm me.

The meal seemed interminable. The Romans, Harry recalled, had installed vomitoriums beside their dining halls in order to allow greater duration to their banquets. What would happen if he should suddenly voice this bit of information at the table? It was inter-esting to think now and then of the outrageous things you *could* say and do, even as you knew you wouldn't. He had considered it in assemblies at school . . . how he could disrupt the whole affair by leaping up to curse the president or yell obscenities in the middle of a speech. From a normal Monday morning gathering of the troops, the ten-fifteen assembly could be reduced to pandemonium, and yet no one ever did it. Probably you'd have to be unbalanced, he decided. He hoped you didn't have to be unbalanced to conceive it. Now, if he supplied his bit of information about the dining habits of Romans . . . Margaret would probably close her eyes and push her plate away. Richard would—what would Richard do? Keep on talking, doubtless.

"That's no lie," Harry said, turning to her. "I am, and I'm going to."

Nan arranged her drawing board on her lap. "Pity I couldn't have brought the easel," she said. "That's right, just drop the hand casually. And don't talk. *Now*," she said, to signify that the moment for argument had passed.

Harry froze in his casual position, and Nan, with brown pastel, began to capture another likeness. There had been dozens this summer. There must be, Harry thought, hundreds, counting last year and the year before, when she had first snared him as a subject. How many had been done of her mother and father overreached comprehension. In the winter, though he didn't see her then—the Gunnings lived in New Jersey, and somehow he and Nan lost track of each other once summer had passed—he understood that she went to nursery schools to sketch children, to parks, to town meetings, to any place that would offer her human figures reasonably still enough for drawing. "Don't you ever bother with anything but people?" he'd asked her. "Why don't you do a portrait of Sam Morely's dog? What's so special about people?" Nan had scarcely listened. "I'm interested in people," she'd replied absently. "But look at this," he'd insisted, handing her a black-and-pink shell, luminous, fragile, delicately convoluted. "This is a beautiful thing. I should think an artist would crow over it. Are any of these people you draw as perfect in their way as this is in its?" "You don't understand," Nan had said. "I want to draw live things." He thought he had her there. "What about Sam's dog?" he demanded. "He's marvelous, and he's certainly alive." Nan shook her head. "Dogs are alive through people," she said. "I want to draw *thinking* aliveness." Well, at any rate, Harry thought, she knows what she wants. Or thinks she does, which amounts to the same thing while you're doing it. The catch usually comes later. He didn't see why Nan should run into a catch, though. She seemed to be at peace with her world, her gift, herself. Not with a placid nodding sort of peace, but with a vibrant capacity to fit, Nan belonged to life and knew what she wanted. Or seemed to. Ah, that word *seem*, Harry thought. What a wingspread it has. The weather seems, the war seems, prices seem, life seems, you seem to me and I to you. But who knows? His mother hadn't seemed to fear death.

Somewhere in *The Life of Samuel Johnson*, Boswell had told a most moving story, one Harry hadn't been able to find again, though he'd tried. Johnson, who had been so terribly afraid of death, had died, and one night Boswell dreamed that the great doctor stood before him. "So, my friend," Boswell said tenderly to the ghost, "at last you've got it over with."

His mother hadn't seemed to be afraid, and yet mustn't anything that has life be afraid to lose it? Never once had she cried out, not once spoken words in a bequeathing way, not once said, "Always remember that I loved you." It must have been hard not to say it. And hadn't they all been brave? Margaret making her cheerful little visits day after day. His father reading aloud late into the night. Himself doing home-

79

work in the big room, looking up now and then to
meet her glance, to talk. His mother had not been
afraid, because if she had been he would have known.
It was afterward they all broke. Afterward that his
father had instituted this strange superintendence over
them. Afterward that Margaret—who would not go to
the funeral—had grown ill and pale with crying, that
he himself had been unable to speak his mother's name
or listen to music. And then, as the months had brought
her death nearer and nearer, so the months took it
farther and farther away. Margaret no longer cried, or
if she did they never knew. Of a Wednesday evening
his father went sedately to dinner at the Yale Club.
You can't follow the people you love into their graves.
But you needn't leave them there either. He had discovered that quite on his own, by going to a concert
one night in late spring and looking at the program
and saying, "Oh, yes, she would have liked this."

He watched the waves heap themselves some distance from the shore. They lifted slowly and then
came in rushing wings of water to break along the
beach. Watching, he could feel how the water gathered beneath you, thrust you up, and bore you gliding
forward. It would be very fine to be in the water rather
than stiffening here in relaxed discomfort for the benefit of Nan Gunning.

"Don't move," she said threateningly.

Or talk, she needn't add. He'd been sufficiently
warned about the dangers of talking. Destroyed the
jawline or the hairline or something. Covertly he

glanced at his wristwatch lying on the sand. Ten minutes to go, if he lasted the proposed half hour. "Now, look here," he'd told her a few days ago, "I found out that *professional* models only pose fifteen minutes, or maybe twenty, and then get a five-minute break." "Yes, but they're getting paid for it," she'd answered tranquilly. Whither logic when Nan pursued her art?

As usual, once he'd stopped wandering about after his own trailing thoughts, he began to be aware of itchings and pains, aware of bits of himself he hadn't even known existed. Where, for instance, was the bone that seemed to be in the calf of his leg? And why hadn't he realized to start with that he was leaning too heavily on his left hand? And, for the love of mud, was there or wasn't there something crawling up his back? He tried a furtive pressure of his hand. If he could push it into the sand a little way, perhaps . . .

"Harry, don't you dare stop yet," Nan pleaded. "I want to catch that expression of pain." She burst out laughing as he turned toward her. "Okay, Harry. Rest."

"You seem to have an imperfect understanding of the word rest," he said, rubbing his back. "If you said, Okay, Harry, collapse, you'd be nearer the truth. I think my circulation's poor. It didn't used to be, see, but it's taken such a beating this year."

"Stop fussing. Here, see if you like it." She handed him the drawing board. She had written in a corner, "Harry, Aet. 17." And there he was, all right. She had a wonderful free sense of line. Nothing cramped or laborious. And the face, barely sketched in, had the pensive look he'd undoubtedly worn.

"Good," he said.

She leaned over to study it. "What were you thinking about?"

"Oh . . . this and that."

She took the drawing board, turned the cover back, and laid it on the sand. "Want to go in the water?"

That was the good thing, one of the good things, about Nan. She never pressed, never pried. "I sure do," he said, and they ran across the sand and hurled themselves into the water, diving through waves, leaping in fans of spray, shouting at each other hoarsely as the cold morning sea swam with them. It was so early that no one had yet come to this far stretch of the beach, which lay beyond meadows uninhabited save for birds and insects nesting in the coarse salt-blown grass. Later in the morning people would begin to drift down. Vigorous types who didn't mind clambering over rocks, who liked the long walk. It was because of the rocks that they hadn't taken Nan's easel. "Oh, you can," Nan had said, standing with him and her father in the kitchen. "A great big strong person like you. You certainly can carry the easel."

"Ah-ah, Nan," Harry had rebuked her. "Flattery doesn't reach me when it's whipped up in a cement mixer."

"It was a little obvious," she said. "But I should think that would make it work. I mean, an obvious person wouldn't be deceived by obvious flattery, but a

subtle person would be taken in by its very obvious-
ness, don't you think?"

"She's doing better, isn't she?" Mr. Gunning had
asked Harry.

"Better, but not good enough. I won't carry the
easel. I hate," he added firmly, "encumbrances." Mr.
Gunning gave him a peculiar glance, but Harry pretended not to see.

Well, later they would begin arriving, the sound of
limb and lung. Meanwhile the beach was his and
Nan's, the rocks with their bouquets of sea lavender,
the meadow with its song birds, the high gull-belled
air, the sloping waters, all theirs. They lay on the
sand again, letting the sun dry their hair and wet
skin. It was gentle at this hour, the sun. As if its
fires were still banked, glowing softly; as if in an
hour or two they would not blaze out in a furnace
heat that would bake the sand, parch the marsh
grasses, and cause umbrellas to flower.

They listened to the bass voice of the ocean, the
treble of gulls and buoys, and then Harry said, "I like
Monday. In the summertime."

"I like it when Daddy's here," Nan said. Not me,
thought Harry, remaining silent. His father had left
last night with Warner, glory be. "It's a funny thing
about my father," Nan mused. "How he changes the
feeling of the house."

"He sure changes the air conditions." Even this
morning, with Mrs. Gunning asleep upstairs, Mr.
Gunning had had his radio going softly, having his

early breakfast before leaving for what would be his last week in the city before vacation.

"Yes, but that's different. I mean that everything seems more alive when he gets here. The radio . . . well, I think that's just a nervous habit. Everybody has them. The way you squeeze your eyes together, for instance."

"Squeeze my eyes together? What are you talking about?"

"Well, you do. It doesn't look bad. Sort of nice, really. Piratical. But a nervous habit just the same."

"You sure know a lot about me."

"Of course I do, Harry," she said softly. There was a moment's silence, and then she said, "Anyway, that's what I meant. About Daddy."

"I see," he answered meditatively. Then, with sudden briskness, "Margaret wants to know if you and I would like to go with her and the ambassador from the Ivy League to a dance Friday night. At the country club. I said I'd ask you."

"Do you want to?"

"It'd be okay. You're a good dancer."

"With such an entreaty, how could I refuse?" He nodded, and appeared to forget the matter.

"I presume the ambassador is **Mr. London?**" she asked.

"Who else?"

"Why do you have it in for him?"

"I don't. He just bores me, and when he's around the house, he bores like an awl. He's like a girl. Can't talk about anything but personalities."

84

"That's certainly a stupid and unoriginal thing to say," Nan snapped.

"Richard? Why he—"

"About girls. What sources of information do you have? How thoroughly have you investigated the conversational patterns of girls that you can sit and proclaim they talk nothing but personalities?"

"Hey, wait a minute. I didn't mean anything—"

"Of course you didn't mean anything. You hadn't thought at all. Any old cliché that comes into your head, out it pops. You were just talking the way boys do, trying to make themselves superior. Do you know something, Harry? When I was in grade school and heard boys saying, 'Aw, girl stuff,' or 'That's just like a girl,' I used to laugh and hope it helped them, because heaven knew they needed help. But *now* . . . I don't think you, of all people, should grab such a feeble prop for your ego. Anyway, I won't help provide it. Who talks personalities more—me or Phil Bowles?"

"Wait, *wait!*" Harry waved his hands. "I'm sorry, I apologize. It was a stupid thing to say and I admit it." When her indignation subsided a little, he repeated, "It was stupid, Nan. And you're right. I said it, you know, the way people do, without thinking."

"*People* I don't mind. But you—"

"I know, Nan. I know. Well," he said with a smile. "Now I promise to consider all clichés before they pop. All right?" She nodded slowly. "Want to do another drawing?"

"Not yet."

She clasped her fingers round her knees, and Harry noticed there were still smudges of brown pastel beneath her nails. Why did that seem rather dear? And why, he wondered, am I in this mood today?

"What are you thinking?" he asked Nan.

"I'm saying to myself 'Andalusia, Portofino, Cairo, Rome.'" She spoke, looking toward the place where sky and sea leaned down, curved up, to meet. "Someday I'm going to travel all over the world," she said dreamily. "They tell me that at night the Alhambra is locked, so you can't go in to hear the nightingales. Isn't that a pity? But you could go in the day, and perhaps at night you could listen near the gates. And Portofino. Doesn't that have a wonderful sound, Harry? So worldly, so poised and wealthy. And in Rome or in Florence . . ." She sighed. "Won't it be wonderful?"

"Maybe."

"What do you mean?" she asked, turning to look in his face.

"Oh— What gives you such confidence?" he burst out. "Why do you think any of those places is even going to be there? Don't you know that the world is headed straight for hell and going faster all the time? What makes you think any of us will be able to travel anywhere? I'll tell you something, Nan. We'll be making our journeys with plasma and guns, not with Baedekers and Brownies, when you and I come to travel."

"Harry," she whispered. "Harry . . . don't."

"My father was talking to me the other day about how I have only one more year before I go to Yale, and shouldn't I jack up my grades—which are perfectly all right anyway, and if they weren't it'd be too late to do a thing about it—and I suddenly thought, What the heck's the use? By the time I'm ready to go to Yale all of New Haven may have been blown to kingdom come."

"You must not talk this way," Nan said tensely. "What's the matter with you today? First you talk like a fool, and now like a . . . a coward. I'm not stupid, and I know how bad everything looks, but things have looked bad before, Harry, and the people who helped were not the ones who sat on the ground and cried. I hate to have someone I—someone I cared for turn out to be one of the snivelers who lies back and says, 'Okay, it's all up, *kill* me.' "

Harry whistled. "You are really in a mood this morning, Teacher." At her impatient gesture, he said, "Nan, look . . . Now, wait a minute, while I figure this out." He frowned at the sand for a long moment and then looked up. "It's like this. You say your father turns on the radio as a nervous mannerism. You admit it seems to calm him, even if no one else sees it that way, right? Well, when I shoot my mouth off like that, I know it's stupid and—craven. But it releases something for me, and then I feel calm, like your father when the guy's singing 'Red River Valley.' Your father isn't even listening most of the time, and I don't mean what I say most of the time, but we both get something out of it. Peace or something. I imagine this sounds pretty thin, but it happens to be true. And besides, of course I'm going to Yale. How would Brooks Brothers stay in business if I and my fellows didn't go to Yale?"

"I'm sorry, Harry," she said in a low voice. "I should have understood."

"You certainly should have," he said sternly. But he reached over to take her hand. "You know, Nan, I'd never talk to anyone else that way because they really wouldn't understand, and I knew you would, eventually, after some of the stupidity had been explained. Tell you another thing. You said just now that you didn't know what was the matter with me today, and yet today I feel . . . happier, and—oh, well, warmer?—than I have in months."

Nan rubbed her eyes. "Harry," she said with a little sob, "you make me feel like a pig."

"Oh, come on," he said, squeezing her hand and letting it go. "How about another drawing? I'll make a special concession and stand on my head for this one. At least I will if you give me a ten-minute break and only a five-minute pose."

Nan tried to smile, pulled her drawing board toward her, and sighed deeply. "If you'll just— Stay the way you are, Harry. That's a good pose." She began to sketch the lines she knew so well, the rather haughty lift of the head, the lazy grace of the powerful limbs, but now she couldn't seem to get them down because of a suspension, a delicate balance in the air between her and Harry, that was not like anything she'd known before, that caused her to breathe with a sort of slow caution and made the beat of her heart so strong that she could feel it hitting at her. Her hand holding the crayon trembled so, and the strangeness within her trembled so. She put the board aside and said softly, "I guess I can't," and lifted her eyes to his. They looked at each other in wonder for a long time.

"Why, I love you," he said incredulously. "I'm in love with you, Nan." And I love you, she answered him without a word. The air vibrated with an almost unbearable brightness before at last they looked away carefully, as though a word or a move might prove it illusion. But what if we hadn't found out? Harry thought. What if this morning hadn't happened just as it has, and we'd gone along not knowing this? It seemed pure chance, and Harry, who always found a way to mistrust fortune, was shaken with apprehension. "Nan," he said, "Nan, don't let anybody know. Don't tell them a thing." She looked at him softly, and he hurried on, "I don't want a lot of people making us seem like—like—"

"No, Harry, we won't let anyone know." She looked down, smiling.

"All right," he said. "Laugh if you will. I don't care if you do. But no one else."

"I don't want to tell. I was just smiling at the way you talk. Nobody else talks the way you do. Nobody sounds like you . . . or looks like you." Her voice sank.

"Nan," he said softly, "don't look like that."

"Like what?"

"You know like what. Anyone could tell. Just see-

89

ing you, they could tell." I'd love to hold you, he thought. I'd love to hold you very close and kiss you. But he looked up and down the beach, knowing that at any moment someone might scramble over the rocks, walk down from the meadows.

"But they could tell by looking at you too," she said.

"Yes. I know." He hadn't noticed before that her eyes had flecks of yellow in the brown. Brown eyes and blond hair. They used to call that turned-about beauty, he'd heard. He hadn't noticed before how clear her voice was, how very beautiful her body. "Nan, please, let's just have this for ourselves."

"Just for us," she told him. They didn't move toward each other or touch, and their love glittered on them like a fall of bright snow.

And yet, Harry thought, when the others had come —Sam and Phil, and Dell Hastings and her cousin Charlie, and Susy Meyers—he and Nan dissembled and did it very well. None of these people they'd known so long noticed anything different in Nan Gunning and Harry Lynch, who were often together but chiefly, they all knew, in the interest of art. None of the parents and nursemaids and children who gradually peopled the sand recognized the presence of joy and love newly sprung this morning. No one noticed or cared. But Harry remembered how people had reacted when Phil Bowles fell in love last summer with the redhead who'd visited the Morelys. Grown-ups had shaken their heads with amusement or frowned

90

in alarm, depending on how closely related they were to Phil and the girl. The other boys, Sam and himself included, had regarded Phil with mildly contemptuous curiosity at his abjectness. The girls had been annoyed with Phil and perhaps a little envious of the redhead. And Phil had been in a pitiful condition, quite unlike his customary joy-*cum*-lust self. Then the girl's parents had whisked her away rather suddenly, and Phil, to all appearances, recovered his aplomb. At any rate he immediately gave Harry and Sam word that his conquest had been extensive, and perhaps it had. But no matter how you looked at it, the thing was too public. Furthermore, Phil and the redhead had been eighteen. When you were even younger they took you both more and less seriously. There would be Phil's insinuations, the prying regard of Sam and Dell and the rest of them. There would be the suddenly alerted attention of the grown-ups. Inescapably someone would say "puppy love," someone else would say "unhealthy," and there would be a blurring of this clear awareness that was Nan's and his alone.

It was as if he'd just awakened, only come alive this morning. Had he ever before felt the steady burning beat of the sun, the drenching collapse of the waves? Had he noticed how voices on the beach and voices in the air mingled, and how now and then one voice would emerge solo and sink again? The sand sucked at his feet as the waves ran out, but had he noticed before how the separate grains swirled and stung, how his heels sank as he leaned against the ocean's strength?

91

And had he ever been able, without a touch or a word or a glance, to feel shaking through him the presence of just one person?

The sun-steeped cloudless day climbed toward its zenith, seemed to hang there motionless, while on the beach brown limbs and gaudy bathing clothes, human voices and tin pails, all tried to possess and make an imprint on the timeless unimpressionable sand. "See," the people and their belongings seemed to say. "See, we're very solid. We'll last." They affirmed themselves with speech and clothing, with love.

Nan lay on her back, her head tilted up a little, eyes closed. She could feel Harry looking at her, and she opened her eyes quickly, and he was. The sound of Dell's voice brought her lids down again and sent Harry running into the water. He was right, they mustn't let the rest know. But she lay, giving him all her love, remembering his eyes.

"Couldn't you do a drawing of me?" Dell asked. "I could give it to Brad."

"Who's Brad?" Nan murmured and didn't listen. The sun was bright against her lids, and she was trying to feel what it would be like when Harry kissed her. I want him to so much, she thought. I never wanted anything so much in my life. I wish all these people would be gone, now, so that Harry could come and sit beside me, lean over me. I would like Harry's hands on me and his lips, I would like his whole self against me, his whole weight on me— But this was what wanting meant, this ache that arched through her body. She sat up suddenly, a little frightened. Even Harry must

92

not guess that, because if he did— But he mustn't.
She wished somehow to cry because wanting Harry
had happened so quickly, with such strange violence,
and they had been carefully reared, the two of them,
firmly instructed as to dangers and honor, the difference between love and desire. All these years they'd
been taught, subtly or frankly, to resist, should it ever
arise, this very emotion. And she didn't even know,
huddling here in the sand, trying to be natural, trying
to smile and talk to Dell and conceal the fact that this
morning she'd left a stage in her life to which she
could never return, she didn't even know, couldn't be
sure, that Harry felt what she did. Maybe she was unnatural, and this was not the way other people their
age fell in love. I don't know what to do with this, she
thought, and for a moment could dislike Harry, swimming out there beyond the reefs, far away from her
and not helping.

"Look, Dell," she said, getting up. "Tell . . . I mean,
if anyone wants to know, tell them I've gone home."

"Something wrong?" Dell asked, watching the tremulous way that Nan gathered her drawing things together.

"No. I mean, I have a sort of stomach ache."

"That's a shame. Want me to walk back with you?"

"*No!* I'm sorry. I just better get off by myself, Dell.
You know how it is."

"Oh, I see," said Dell, thinking she did. "You
shouldn't have come out here this morning at all in
that case."

Nan picked up her towel. "Perhaps not," she said

dully and began walking down the long beach, not once looking out to sea.

Harry was a better swimmer than Phil and had soon outdistanced him, so that now, beyond the reefs, he was alone and safe from Phil's crafty regard. The guy roots like a pig after truffles, Harry thought angrily, driving through the water with long smashing strokes.

"Nan looks pretty . . . mellow this A.M.," Phil had said as he and Harry went down to the water. "You have anything to do with that?"

Harry had stiffened but kept walking. "What do you mean by that?" he'd asked when Phil's silence became too pointed.

"Nothing. Just remarking."

You'll remark yourself into a black eye one of these days, Harry thought. He said, "I didn't notice she was any different."

"Oh, well, if you didn't," Phil said, and then apparently lost interest. "Did you ask your father about—"

"No." Harry dove into the water and started swimming away from that voice, away and away till he felt free. Then he relaxed on the sea's breathing depth.

Maybe at that—he rolled to his back and floated half submerged—maybe at that Phil hadn't meant anything. You just got used to thinking of Phil's every remark as an allusion to sex. Even if it had been, what difference did it make? Phil could guess, and no one could stop him from making his guesses suggestive, but he couldn't know. What Nan and I have, thought proud Harry, is nothing Phil Bowles could understand. He squinted at the great sky above him, and what he really thought was that no one could understand, and he was glad of it.

He swam back lazily. She would be there, and everything about her, every gesture, every word, would be secret and important and meant for him. But there was all this day to go through, with all these people, before tonight came. Even in the cold path of the ocean he felt the dizzying warmth of the knowledge that he could kiss Nan tonight.

But when he came out of the water, dripping and exultant, he couldn't see her. Looking up and down the beach, quickly out at the bathers, he saw no sign of her anywhere, and because he'd been so sure of her presence, so certain of her being here to meet his eyes after his long swim, his disappointment flared without proportion. All that wonder and mystery made tangible this morning—so she could just walk away from it, could she? Just pack up when he wasn't looking and go along for lunch or a bit of a chat with her mother or some other everyday matter, as if this were not a different day, a day like no other, and not to be shared with anyone but him? Resentful, then suddenly desolate, he stood at the water's edge, wondering why he couldn't believe enough in either himself or Nan to know that this was not desertion. An hour ago there'd been nothing so real in the world as this new love, but could they say they were in love if Nan wouldn't wait for him and he wouldn't understand when she didn't? And if they weren't in love, what had they been talking about and feeling? And if they weren't in love, what mattered anyway now? Like showing you in one great flash the architecture of heaven and then saying, Wonderful, isn't it? But not for you. Sorry, but not for you.

"Harry, my boy?"

"What is it?" he snapped at Sam, who looked at him and shrugged and walked away. Harry looked after him uncertainly. Oh, well, he'd patch it up later. Right now he couldn't care. Right now he couldn't figure a move to make. Only to stand here between the sea and the beach, becalmed, with no aim. Why had she left? She couldn't have changed her mind. Could she have? Had he frightened her? But that wasn't true. They'd both been a little frightened, but it had been a wonderful feeling, the sort of glorious fear you know at the top of a precipice, leaning over the sheer verticals of rocks, gazing at clouds of leaves far, far below, wondering what if . . . But you aren't really *afraid*.

And what do we do now? he wondered. What is this supposed to mean? He walked heavily up the beach to sit with the others.

"What's the matter with everyone today?" Dell asked. She'd been lying with an arm crooked across her eyes, but now she sat up impatiently.

"Is something the matter?" Susy Meyers wondered. "I hadn't noticed."

"Well, I think we're acting like a lot of zombies," Dell said. "Sam and Harry here. And Nan took off all of a sudden, looking like the queen of death maidens.

96

Of course," she added contritely, "she didn't feel good, but just the same . . ."

Sick? Harry thought. But she couldn't be. She was—
"She sick?" Susy said.

Dell flushed and answered, "Oh, tired or something," and asked Charlie if he wouldn't like to swim.

As they all stood up Phil said, "Well, sick or no, that Nan's beginning to have something, and if she gets just a little more of it, that's for me."

His words were still a presence in the air when Harry's fist crashed against his jaw. The blow was not expert or heavy, but Phil went down quickly because neither of them had used fists for fighting since they'd left grade school. But the emotional impact was momentarily overwhelming. Heads turned and eyes stared, and there were outcries from all sides. Susy Meyers put her hands over her face, Dell looked frankly excited, Charlie and Sam tensely expectant. But Phil, maddeningly, unreasonably, was not angry. He sat in the sand looking at Harry with an astounded expression, and Harry stood looking down at him with no expression at all.

Phil got to his feet. "Harry," he said, "what's the matter with you?"

It was not what Harry expected, a long way from what he wanted. He wanted to fight Phil there on the spot till they both fell smashed and bleeding, senseless if possible. Phil's words shuffled his mood apart, left him frustrated, angrily aware of having revealed Nan and himself to these people, uncertain whether what he'd revealed was true any longer. Phil's casual rejection of the glove made Harry ludicrous in the eyes of these people nearby (who, seeing there was to be no contest where one had been promised, exchanged glances of brief amusement and turned away), put him in a strangely disreputable light before these, his friends. Made him, in short, an ass. There was an embarrassed pause before he relaxed his clenched fists and said, "Sorry." But they didn't know what he was sorry about.

The militant moment spent, Harry didn't leave as he wished to, and no one mentioned Nan again. Until lunchtime they played in the water, lay on the sand, talked to each other with calculated lightness. The summer-browned youngsters riding the crest of what their parents (because of short or nervous memories) thought of as the carefree time of life.

Chapter 5

THE SUN, a fiery fellow at the beach, a sullen, heavy presence in the city, was a true gentleman at the club.

At the pool the light was full and hot, but blue sparkling water, fringed umbrellas cocked to shadow limbs and tables, frosty glasses brought by white-jacketed waiters—all functioned as sun diffusers.

". . . when she said, I know my husband and I trust him, I thought I'd *drop*, but of course when you think it over, it's sort of pathetic. . . ."

"At . . . William and Mary, and honestly the most gorgeous creatures; I don't think I saw a man under six feet. . . ."

"Mother says she doesn't, but I *know* she waits up at night and it gives you this sort of spied-on feeling with nothing in the world to do about it, you know what I mean?"

". . . and I really wanted to nurse the baby, I told them so, but they say I'm too high-strung, and anyway I guess it would have ruined my figure. . . ."

Margaret thought, This is what Dad means when he says we all talk tripe. Not, in the three hours we've been here, one serious or thoughtful remark. On the other hand I'd like to hear Dad and his cohorts at Marburg, Lynch and Porter when they aren't discussing business. Do *they* speak seriously and thoughtfully? Do they wonder aloud about right and wrong, about man and his fate? Do they speak to each other, as Harry sometimes speaks to me—used to speak to me—of music, of books? I don't think they do. I think they kick the government around the way people do here, and when they get tired of that, kick their acquaintances around. I think they talk about themselves all the time, just the way we do. I, I, I, says Mr. Marburg, while Daddy is trying to say I, I, I louder than Mr. Porter can. Who's he to say "shut up" to Richard?

She reclined in a low canvas beach chair, one hand holding a cigarette, the other idly clasping a tepid gin rickey. She wore dark glasses, a little white piqué hat on her dark curling hair, an expensive simple cotton swimsuit. She looked what she was, a daughter of privilege. What's more, she thought, I like it. I've compounded no injustice. Injustice, prerogatives, those have always existed. I was lucky enough to be born on the prerogative side, so what am I supposed to do . . . cast my luck aside and go to live and work among the squalid unlucky? *Nobody asked you, dear, he said.* That's right. No one had ever suggested such a thing. Why then was she (and she, it seemed, alone of all the people she knew) tormented by unease? Why did she have to close her eyes when Warner drove them through the outlying streets of the city where tough, dirty children yelled remarks at their passing car, where tired wretchedly made-up girls looked up with sudden sullen wistfulness, where skulking scabby animals peered out of alleyways? Why did she refuse to do any charity work, the way the other girls in the League did? It was obvious that she was either going to have to do some or quit the League. It was also obvious that she'd quit before she'd do volunteer work or donate several hours a week to a hospital or write letters for the blind. I intend, she told herself, to close my eyes and keep them closed until they can be safely opened on such a scene as this. With Richard beside her.

She'd met Richard at the Debutante Cotillion, the night she came out. Mother had considered the whole business of coming out pretty silly. "It's obvious," she had said, "that those of our ancestors who wanted a king are not without descendants."

"It isn't that at all," seventeen-year-old Margaret had said. "It's fun. And all my friends will be doing it. And anyway, it can be very, very vital in a girl's life."

"Which of your friends' mothers are you quoting

now?" Mother had asked, and Margaret hadn't answered because she'd been quoting several of them. "If you really want to, naturally we'll see that you do," Mother had gone on to say. "I'm only trying to point out to you that in America such a thing is archaic, or should be. There are no real social distinctions left in our country, thank heaven, and these affairs are simply attempts to draw a line where no line can be drawn, or anyway, nothing much more than a squiggle."

"*You* came out."

"So I did," Katherine had said remotely. "All right, love, what would you like to wear?"

And it had been fun, in spite of Mother's carping, in spite of Dad's reluctance to be involved. "Me?" he'd said. "What do I have to do with it besides foot the bill? Which I'm happy to do," he hurried on, as Margaret showed signs of tearful enragement.

"Now, Henry," Mother had said soothingly. "You needn't get there till late if you don't wish to. But the girls enter on their fathers' arms at midnight and make their bows, and Margaret is going to enter on yours."

"Is that all?" he'd asked grumpily.

"Just about. You dance a few steps with her, and then some boy will relieve you of the chore." But Dad, with one of his unexpected reversals of character, had been charming and even mildly annoyed when, after the bows to the patronesses, he'd taken Margaret in his arms for the formal figure and had been cut in on before they'd moved three steps.

It wasn't one of the two boys she'd invited who cut in. It was Richard. Older than her escorts. There were always these older men, who came with the post-debs or stag for the drinks. Richard had been so beautiful in his beautiful clothes, but she'd only had a chance to smile at him with happy surprise before her outraged Andover boy appeared with a firm shoulder tap and a remark to Margaret about old men sticking to their old bags. And then her Groton boy had replaced Andover, and then others came and others, some she knew, some she didn't; and it was all a tranced adorable whirl, during which, every now and then, she caught Richard's eye upon her, warm, admiring, amused at her fun. Oh, a lovely night, ending, after scrambled eggs and coffee, with tumbling into sleep in her sunlit bedroom, her dress (with the hem ripped) thrown across a chair, her shoes (wrecked, like the shoes of the Twelve Dancing Princesses) tossed in a corner, her corsage (quite brown and withered) pressed between *All Countries* and *The Feudal Ages* in a volume of her long unused *Book of Knowledge*. It was still there.

She hadn't seen Richard again until last March. And she couldn't honestly say that she'd thought about him, except for the first week or so after the Cotillion. There'd been something so romantic in this stranger's appearance, in his brief holding of her, that she could not help dwelling on a certain hope that he might send a single rose, or telephone from New Orleans and say, "Fly to me," or make some picturesque unlikely move, as if they were both characters in a play. However, he hadn't, and she had had to think a moment on that warm March day, just outside the

Plaza, when the young man smiled and said, "Hello, Miss Lynch. Still dancing?"

"Dancing?" she'd echoed uncertainly. And then, "Oh, hello. It's you."

"So it is. How did you remember?"

Margaret had lowered her eyes. "I didn't forget," she said softly. "I thought for a while that you'd call me, or—do something about me."

By now, months later, kisses and vows later, they quite believed that the intervening years between the ball and their remeeting had been spent in endless yearning for each other, though Richard in those years had been engaged once and Margaret had been to college and pinned three times. Richard was the easiest person to be with that Margaret had ever known. He was well-to-do, devoted, and elegant. He loved her but never frightened her with depths of passion. He was intelligent, but there were no complications in him. Richard could shrug about anything or laugh. Make anything easy to bear. Her father, she knew, considered him a fool. But that wasn't so. Neither a fool nor a clown. A courtier. An attendant lord. And they were very decorative, very necessary . . . "to swell a sentence, start a scene or two." They could also be a lot of fun and comfort for people less agonized and thought-consumed than Hamlet. The point isn't that we can't all be Prince Hamlet, Margaret thought, it's that just about none of us can. But we're alive. We have to feel and do things and wonder now and then *Who am I? Who is that?* I'd rather be an attendant lady, only required to circle and laugh and whisper *one, two, three* in someone's ear, than be Ophelia, who was very, very special but could not choose but weep—and drown. I do not choose to drown. Not in a flower-crusted brook, nor in thought, nor in love. I shall walk beside the brook with my lord, laughing and talking lightly, thinking little or not at all, loving happily. And make no mistake, she mentally told her father, I love Richard. But an attendant lord would never make you unhappy, because he'd never be unhappy himself. *Would he?*

"Penny for them," Richard said now, putting his hand under her chin, turning her face toward him.

"Hand it over."

He reached into his robe pocket, shook his head. "Cigarettes, lighter, keys, no dough."

"Well, for free then, I was thinking I'd like lunch. It's after two o'clock."

At the club a buffet lunch was served daily at the pool. It was set up in a luxurious lean-to, screened and frolicksomely decorated. Cold lobster, ham, turkey, beef, salad, and hot casseroles, relishes and rolls, desserts, coffee and tea, hot or iced. You could get a waiter to fill your tray, but generally the club members liked to saunter around the pool, enter the lean-to, and serve themselves. It seemed to them that if you weren't ill or utterly exhausted from the morning, you could certainly get up and attend to your own lunch.

Margaret took off her glasses, her little hat, pulled on a bathing cap. "I'll have one more paddle," she told Richard and dived into the pool. The breeze came from the ocean on one side, from the meadows and pine woods on the other, the pool water swayed against blue tile, and Margaret went smoothly, lifting her glistening brown arms, toward the deep end while Richard in his cork shoes walked to meet her, smiling fondly.

When they were at their table, lunches arranged before them, Johnny Frost and Cicely Harmer, his current girl, came to join them. Johnny had a little gray leather portable radio turned low. He set it beside him on the board floor and scowled at it briefly before settling to his food.

". . . and it's a, no . . . yes it *is, it is* another great hit by Mickey Mantle! Man, what a powerhouse. . . ."

Johnny leaned over and snapped off the radio as though he were snapping his fingers in the announcer's face. "That guy oughta be thrown off the air," he growled, attacking a mold of lobster mayonnaise. "You'd think no one in the whole country was playing ball except Mickey Mantle."

Margaret and Cicely exchanged glances, and Richard said, "Oh, well, he's always been like that. Even when DiMaggio was falling all over his own feet, no one could fall over his feet like DiMaggio."

"It's unethical, that's what it is," Johnny said. "I hope they get their pants trounced off, bunch of bores. Always right, never wrong. And if they were ever wrong, how'd anybody know with that publicity man at the mike?"

"I didn't get any lemon with my iced tea," Cicely said mildly.

Johnny gave her an exasperated glance but got to his feet. "Anyone else want anything while I'm at it?"

"You might bring me a couple more rolls," Richard said. "And if you see that waiter, tell him I'd like another gin rickey. How about you?" he said to Margaret and Cicely. "Like a drink?" They didn't think they would just yet. Johnny went off in long strides, enraged with Mickey Mantle, with Mel Allen, with the world.

"I just don't see all that adrenalin or whatever it is being wasted on baseball," Cicely commented, looking after him. "A lot of men playing a kid's game, and the whole country goes crazy."

"Well, if you don't understand, you don't," Richard said. "But it isn't a lot of men playing a kid's game, it's a . . . a symbol, in a way. Like the marathons in Greece, or the tournaments in the Middle Ages. Those runners and those jousters were not just themselves, they were running and jousting for all the people who wanted to but couldn't do it. They were . . . representatives of man's sporting instinct."

"I hate games, baseball and all the rest. Just another way of trying to beat somebody up. Or out," Cicely said.

"Still, it's all very human," Richard persisted.

"Is that supposed to make it all right?" Cicely asked with a bitter note that brought Margaret's notice to the conversation she'd been almost ignoring. What, she wondered, was Cicely's trouble? "As far as I'm concerned," Cicely went on, "the best thing that could happen to all of us 'very humans' is to have Halley's comet turn around and smash right through us this minute."

"Do you mean to say," Richard asked sharply, "that you'd take upon yourself the responsibility for the annihilation of the whole human race?"

"Listen, if Halley's comet hit us, it wouldn't be the human race, it'd be the whole shooting match. *Poof*, and no more world. Just a bit of space in all that space." Cicely looked directly at Richard. "And, yes, I'd take the responsibility."

"Well, that's damned high-handed," Richard said, and Margaret burst out laughing.

On the terrace Johnny Frost was standing with Mitzi Clavering. They looked laughingly intimate and once glanced over at Cicely in a speculative way. Then they talked earnestly, Johnny making a lot of gestures, Mitzi shrugging from time to time. Cicely never took her eyes from them.

Margaret felt sorry for Cicely, but at the same time it was laughable. In order to keep Mitzi from annexing Johnny, Cicely was prepared to do away with everyone and everything from kings and presidents to some small insect feeling its way through the bottom of a Philippine jungle. *What large emotions you have, Grandma,* she murmured to herself.

When the waiter came with Richard's drink, and another appeared to clear the table, Margaret returned to her low beach chair, turning it now to face the sun, and lay back with her eyes closed. Once in a while you got tired of looking at things, of looking at people, even things and people as attractively designed

as these around her. Tired of the beautiful unhappy,
the beautiful predatory, the beautiful unthinking.
Tired even of the beautiful gay, and the absolutely
beautiful décor.

She moved restlessly. What are we going to do all
afternoon? What, for that matter, are we going to do
for the rest of this vacation? Spend every waking hour
at this club? Monday afternoon and practically a
month to go. It wasn't that she didn't adore having
Richard with her. Having him was what she wanted
above everything else. Only what in the world were
they going to do?

By eight in the evening the tide was out. So far had
the ocean retreated that it would be a matter for wonder, had this miracle not become commonplace, to consider how in a few hours' time that distant water line
would return upon the shore, all those swirling sand-
bars be engulfed, the leggy stranded pier and massive
rocks be mantled once again. Now the rocks started up
blackly against the flaming sky, and the seaweed
dripped across them like disordered hair. You could
see the wild sunset through the understructure of the
pier. But all the color in the sky could not make the
ebb tide anything but frightening, a tremendous desertion that the land would always forgive and never
forget.

There were no people on the beach. A crane flew
overhead, long neck out, long legs trailing. A large
brown turtle went with ponderous rhythm across the
sand, a host of tiny crabs jittering sideways in his

wake, and the seagulls came on bent wings to roost upon the rocks.

Harry came out of his house just as the day, with a dying flare, fell behind the rim of the ocean. He stood watching the swift dissolution of green and crimson from the sky, then stood a little longer in the dusk where the only shadows were close to the house because the only light was there. Farther, even just so far as the rose arbor, there was nothing now but darkness, and would not be until the moon rose. He glanced through the window at the living room, gently lit and empty, all the down cushions still uncrushed, the flowers bright in their porcelain bowls. Aggie had gone in to turn the lights on, but otherwise there hadn't been anyone in the living room all day. Upstairs, above the porch, Margaret had the radio on in her room and the music came through the square glow of her window softly, without insistence, something to have and not listen to as she dressed for dancing. How she dances, Harry thought. How she does go on and on dancing. Richard presumably was in his room getting into a dinner jacket, and Aggie was finishing up the kitchen with Warner, who'd gotten back just before dinner. Harry lingered, thinking about the Warners. Why did some people seem to belong together, as if any other way were impossible? They were born and spent a little time growing up, but the essence all along had been their coming together, joining, proceeding as one. The twoness that Margaret and Richard had displayed was not the same thing at all. And there was, Harry thought, an absolute one and one dividedness between my mother and father. The Gunnings seemed very happy together but not inevitable. The only two people he could ever think of as *one* were the Warners, and he couldn't understand why. You never saw Warner seek out his wife's eyes, as Richard constantly sought Margaret's. You never heard Aggie compliment her husband, the way Mrs. Gunning so charmingly did hers. With the Warners, Harry thought perplexedly, it would be like complimenting yourself or looking in a mirror to meet your own eyes.

This morning he and Nan, in that exalted, nearly wordless hour, had seemed like one, had seemed inescapably to have arrived at a place no less decreed than the place of the moon at a given hour. And now what? All the long rest of the day with no sight of her, no word from her. Why had she left, and why had she stayed away all day, and why had he done nothing about it but suffer and stay away too? *Love,* he thought bitterly. We decided it was love. Well, if it was, it's distinguished itself by being one of the shortest loves in history. Only I don't believe it. A thing doesn't happen like that and then just—disintegrate. What happened? What did I do to her to make her go away like that without a word, without waiting a little time till I came back? She could have come down to the water to meet me and say what was wrong, to let me talk to her.

The breath ached in his chest and his eyes looking into the dark were desolate. She changed her mind, that's all. One minute she did, next minute she didn't. Simple as that. And she didn't have the nerve to tell me. A thought, incompletely comprehended, crossed his consciousness and buried itself: *That's what women always do, make you love them and then leave you without a word.* Okay, he said. Okay. I don't give a damn about any of it. He formed these sentences in his mind, expecting them to make him feel better, and then suddenly bolted into the night as Margaret, in her room, began to sing: "Alas, my love, you do me wrong . . . to treat me so discourteously. . . ."

His soft shoes made little sound on the dirt road, though insect voices in the grass beside him stilled at his approach and welled again as he passed. From the various houses came normal evening sounds: creaking of porch gliders, intermittent conversations, television programs, names suddenly called out, garden sprays whirling on dark lawns, children wheedling or protesting. You'd think it all meant something, thought the boy walking on the road. You'd think the lawn sprinklers and the panel shows and the question of what time you go to bed now that you're eight years old really mattered, when of course none of it matters at all. Take a look at the sky, a look at a grave, and you see how completely it is not important. Whether your heart or the picture tube in your television set breaks, it comes to the same thing, which is nothing.

He swung with youth's great facile inconsistency from everything to nothing, and like a child on a huge mechanical fairground swing, could only hold on and go with it, not able to regret having gotten on, not able to conceive of its ever stopping. Just to cling as it raced forward, hurtled down, sped up and backward . . . just to hold on as his world—flat and solid so little time ago—reared and wheeled past him in a light-streaked wall. There, in a flash of trailing white, went his mother, heedless of him as that trailing heron; there went Margaret and Aggie, speeding away like comets and speeding back; down came his father like a spent rocket; and spiraling away, never getting away, always impelled away, was Nan.

For a moment Harry halted in the middle of the road, swallowing hard against a desire to put his head down on something and cry. Then he took a long breath, put his hands in his pockets, and resumed his walk. He was whistling "Greensleeves" softly as he turned into the Gunnings' back yard, and when Mrs. Gunning on the porch said, "Hello, Harry, where've you been all day?" he answered easily, "Around and about, Mrs. Gunning. Around and about."

"Come and sit down," she invited. "Isn't it a grand night? Should be a moon, I think, in a little while."

"Unless the world is ending, there'll be a moon tonight."

Mrs. Gunning smiled. "Is that poetry? I mean, are you quoting something?"

"I don't think so," Harry said, sitting on the topmost step, turning to look through the screen door. Be darned if I'll say it, he told himself, and said, "Where's Nan?"

"Nan's gone crazy," Mrs. Gunning answered with something like a chuckle. "She came in this morning and started housecleaning and she's been at it ever since. Washed down all the kitchen shelves, the cellar steps, the back porch. I tried to keep up, though it was certainly nothing I'd *planned* to do. After all, in another few weeks we'll have to do the fall cleaning up"—Harry's stomach contracted a little at this easy reference to the summer's end, but Mrs. Gunning went on—"so doing it now is just an extra bit of work in the middle that won't count for much. But you can't stop Nan when she's being energetic." She laughed softly again and then said, "I left her because I was too limp even to watch anymore, and then she was scrubbing every pot and pan in the kitchen. To go with her clean shelves, I guess. Run along, dear. You'll find her drudging in the scullery."

Because it would seem odd if he didn't, Harry got up and started for the kitchen. He was reluctant now and wished he hadn't come, or that Nan had been sitting on the porch with her mother so that he wouldn't have had to see her alone. His pulse was heavy in his throat, and he wasn't sure he'd be able to speak at all. A light in the kitchen, a vigorous tinny scrubbing, told him that she was working all right. He approached the door with a feeling of dread and one backward glance at the porch and Mrs. Gunning.

Cinderella in blue jeans. Her back was toward him, and as he saw her she raised an arm, hand gripping a steel-wool brush, to shove her hair back and remained that way a moment, arm up, back arched. She's so beautiful, Harry thought. When he spoke she started and spun around with a little cry. Then, too brightly, she said, "Hi, Harry. You frightened me."

"I'm sorry."

They looked at each other in silence, breathing quickly, lightly.

"Cleaning up, I see," Harry said, just as she said, "Doing a little housework, don't ask me why."

Another moment passed during which neither spoke, and then with a little smile, Nan said, "Yes. Cleaning up. I'll be through in a minute."

"Don't hurry for me. I mean, I have nothing to do. I could help maybe."

"Oh, no. You needn't work in the kitchen every time you come here." Since that referred to a morning when they'd still been on their old easy basis, she flushed and turned back to the sink. "I'll just finish this thing and straighten up. Then we . . . we can sit on the porch with Mother. Have lemonade or something."

Harry leaned against the door jamb. I'm not going to ask to be alone with you, he thought. If you want to sit with your mother . . . so we'll sit with your mother.

"What did you do?" he burst out with sudden irrepressible harshness. "Just suddenly remember as you sat on the sand that the kitchen needed cleaning?" Nan shook her lowered head, not answering. "It sure must have been in some condition," Harry pursued, trying, with no success, to keep the hurt out of his voice, "to send you haring off to the Brillo without a word to anybody. And why did you tell them you were sick? If you're off to do a spot of housecleaning, that's nothing to be ashamed of. Say it right out. 'I'm going to clean my kitchen.' Say it. Shout it from the house-tops. Nobody's going to think there's anything wrong with cleaning the kitchen. You don't have to announce a sudden bellyache just to get away—"

"Harry, *stop it,*" she cried, turning to face him, her fist against her mouth, her eyes wide. "Stop it."

"Stop it? Sure I'll stop it. I'll stop any darned old thing you want me to. If you can stop things like— things—" He broke off. "Speaking of stopping things, you'd better tell your friends tomorrow that I'm just an impulsive boy and nothing to do with you, because I knocked Phil Bowles down and practically told them that we—that—" Again the words caught in his throat.

"Knocked him down?" Nan said faintly.

"Oh, nothing dashing. He was so surprised he fell down, and then he wouldn't do a thing about it. Laughed at me, really."

"Harry," she whispered. "Harry—"

"I'm not interested in that," he said impatiently. "I'm just trying to tell you that if you wish to correct an apparently completely wrong impression, you'd better get at it tomorrow."

A big moth blundered against the screen and tried and tried, crawling up and down, to find a way into the kitchen. A bicycle horn sounded outside. Swift skidding drops fell from the faucet to the upturned pot in the sink, plinking and streaming as Harry became aware of Nan's face, of its stunned, still unhappiness, of the large silent tears pouring over her smudgy cheeks. "Ah, Nan," he said hoarsely. "Nan, I didn't mean it—"

"I know you didn't," she whispered. "It's just . . . Harry, I—"

They heard the rocker on the front porch creak, the slight preliminary sound of Mrs. Gunning preparing to enter the house. Nan took huge gulping breaths, blew her nose, and said, "Tell Mom I'll be right down." She ran up the back stairs, leaving Harry to compose and lighten his face in the moment that was left. Mrs. Gunning found him at the sink, grinding away with the steel wool.

"My word, she certainly put you to work fast."

"Sure did."

"Harry, dear, that pot is now clean." She moved over beside him, looking not in his face but in the sink, awash with gray tepid water. "I do think it's time to call a halt. Where's Nan?"

"Upstairs. Said she'd be down in a minute."

"Well, suppose you let me take over here now. When Nan comes down, I'll tell her to see you on the porch. Then we can all have some lemonade."

Mrs. Gunning, Harry thought, is a very nice woman. It was not her fault that she failed to recognize so much suppressed emotion in a pair of people—pair of kids, in her eyes—who'd never had anything in relation to each other to suppress before. They sat on the porch, the three of them, and Mrs. Gunning talked in a low voice, laughed gently at Nan's industry, rocked peacefully.

"You went at it too hard, love," she told Nan, who was sitting across from Harry on the top step, drinking lemonade and staring into the darkness, only rousing herself now and then to make an almost demanded reply.

And now there came the moon, full and pure, lifting itself easily over the entangling dark boughs of the trees.

"There it is," said Mrs. Gunning.

Harry nodded and put his glass beside him. "Would it be okay if Nan and I walked down to the pavilion?"

"That would be nice," Nan said after a pause.

"You're sure you aren't too tired?" her mother asked but without urgency, and Nan shook her head. Mrs. Gunning, looking after them as they went down the walk and away, so scrupulously not near each other, knew a feeling she hadn't had before about Nan. It took her a little while to identify it. Loss, she thought. I'm losing her. There had been all these years of protection, of closeness, of—though she'd read enough of psychology to deplore the term—possession. In some way, psychologists aside, she'd possessed Nan until tonight. She remembered her young self, with Nan only a baby, saying in earnest to young Bert, her husband, who did not agree at all, "We must never think we *own* her, always remember that she's her own person, always remember that when the time comes . . ." But they had smiled at each other because Nan was a baby, and they were young, and there was all of time before them, so how could *that* time come?

And now it has, thought Mrs. Gunning (no longer young but certainly not old). Now it has. And what do I do? She sat in her rocker, looking at what she could no longer see, wishing her husband were with her, and realized that of course she did nothing at all. How well they hide things, she thought. What natural, if desperate, disguises they assume. Poor children, how little they would like her knowing. Yet it was nothing she had sought to know, expected to know. For all that what's-his-name, that sour malcontent, had to say about Moms, there remained to mothers this rather unwelcome intuition. What they did when it spoke was what made or broke his thesis. She imagined there were a great many who did just what she would. Nothing. Always hoping that good would come to this special person no longer their own.

And at that, having Bert would not have helped except as it helps to have to comfort others. Bert, unalterably opposed to Nan's growing up and blind to symptoms, was going to find this a bitter surprise when he arrived for his vacation. He would come joyfully shedding problems of business and the city, problems of the man of small business, prepared to spend these two weeks in the constant company of his wife and child. He would have fishing expeditions and outdoor grills and three-handed card games buzzing brightly in his mind . . . because that was the way it had always been. Mrs. Gunning was drained by the knowledge that their days of three-sided play were over, that Bert had still to learn it. He would try his best, and it would be a good best, to accept what she was accepting now, the fact that suddenly Nan was not, and never would be again, a real part of their family. He'd try. She had no hope at all that his muffled pained resentment would not make itself known, that his hurt resistance to change would not in turn hurt all of them.

You can't really talk to anyone, she thought. Or maybe some people can, but most of us make do with surface words, skimmed reactions. Averted eyes and dissembling tones seem to make reality easier for us to bear. Why wouldn't I say, "Listen to me, Bert. I know you're sick with pain and jealousy, with fear of growing old. I know you've loved Nan more than you should and that you're suffering now almost more than you can bear. But, darling, can't you, if you try, turn back to me now? You and I are young. We could have a lovely life together, as we had long ago, before she was born. Bert, let's go back to that time, a little wiser, together." Well, it was all true enough. A trifle dramatic, a trifle maudlin, but common truths were often that. It was nothing she would say to Bert, who'd look ashamed or annoyed or simply blank. Who'd say, "What are you talking about, Martha? Make sense, will you?" and go back to his radio or his carpentry, signifying by his silence that what he ignored either hadn't happened or was not important.

A good, devoted man, a husband to cherish, her Bert. It was no more his failing than hers that they could not and never had been able to speak to each other. And perhaps some feelings are better left unsaid. Once you've given them shape in words— fear, sorrow, and, yes, hatred—you can't destroy them. Better, she told herself, to keep them hidden, unformed by sound, shapeless. Then you can always

120

pretend that they really don't exist, or are matter so amorphous that any words or no words would serve them just as well. This time that lay ahead of them, this time of Nan's assuming her inescapable role of adulthood, was not going to be simple, because the various stages of life are not arrived at unnoticeably or even smoothly. But the three of them, like so many others, could be relied upon to make the change as easy as possible by deliberate blindness and deliberate evasion.

I wonder, she thought suddenly, if Nan and Harry can talk to each other?

The pavilion, vacant, dark, strange at night as it was never strange in the daytime, did not welcome them. The seats were hard, the wide-board floor sand-drifted, unkindly shadowed. And the beach looked queer and unpleasant to Nan. How could you ever believe it golden, or erupting with people, with color and voices? It lay so still, so flat and dark. The sound of the ocean was a distant *shussh*. Sitting stiffly next to Harry on a bench beside the front rail, she shivered and said, "I don't like it tonight. Some nights I do, but now—"

"Because the tide is out," he said.

"Maybe that's it."

They sat unmoving for a little time, and then Harry said, "Aren't you going to tell me what happened?" Even in the dark he didn't look at her.

"I got frightened."

"Of me?"

"I don't know, Harry. Of both of us, I suppose. Or

maybe just of me." She laced her fingers together, played without noticing, *This is the church, this is the steeple, open the door and see the people.* When she'd done it twice, she pulled her hands apart abruptly. "Silly," she said with a little laugh. "Child's game."

"What's a child's game?" he asked, uncertain, ready to be offended.

Nan said quickly, "I didn't mean us, Harry. I meant, I was playing that kid's game, This is the church, this is—" She sighed, giving up.

"I wonder why we're so suspicious of each other," Harry said. "We didn't used to be."

"No, we didn't used to be. Only . . . it's different now. I mean, we are."

Harry felt again a thick pounding in his throat. Just her saying it could set his blood coursing this way. Just her admission, with only the two of them to hear, in the dark, that something had changed between them. And they knew what.

You don't go back, Harry thought. You can't, but you wouldn't anyway. Yet there were times when you couldn't go forward either. Oh, God, he thought, I wish we were ten years older or even five years. He felt so trapped, here at this age, so ignorant and clumsy and uncertain. Was she thinking what he was? What did he mean? *they knew what.* How did he know what Nan this moment was feeling or wanting? Just for him to kiss her? And saying *just* . . . what did he mean by that? Oh, who do you think you're fooling, he asked himself. You may not know what's in her mind, but you know what's in yours. Over the tremendous pumping of his heart his mind said, That's Nan you're talking about. Nan, whom you've known forever. She's sixteen years old.

He said quietly, "Nan, you don't have to be frightened. I won't . . . I mean, we won't . . ." He swallowed, tightening his fists on the rail before him.

"But I want you to. I want it."

He thought for a shocked, suspended moment that he hadn't heard right.

Then he groaned and put his head down on his clenched fists, thinking, There'll never be anything harder than this. This is the hardest thing I'll ever have to do. Savagely hard to have to think for and fight just himself, but to have to do it for both of them. . . . Oh, Nan, Nan darling, he thought. When somebody does, let it be me. When somebody has you . . .

He felt a sudden tentative touch on his shoulder. "Harry?" she asked, and he could barely hear her. "Harry? Are you mad at me?"

For some reason, he didn't know why, her single whispered question sent the tumult out of his blood, and he could smile, because she was so sweet and so young. He sat up and turned to her and said, "I'll never be mad at you. I'll never be anything but in love with you, all my life."

"I see," she said softly. "I thought . . . I meant that, Harry. You'll have to know that I meant it."

"I do know. Just the way we both know . . . we can't. You're sixteen years old, Nan. What kind of a guy do you think I am?" Her eyes in the dark made it clear what she thought he was. She had no reservations. He put his arms around her, gently at first and then harder as their lips met in their first kiss. No one, he told her wordlessly, with a sort of wild protectiveness, no one has ever loved anyone as much as I love you. He kissed her ear and her hair, and he told her over and over.

Nan drew away a little, looking at him curiously. "Harry," she said. "Have you ever?"

"Ever what? Oh . . ." He shook his head. "No. I haven't even thought about it." He gazed over her head and added, "Well, I have . . . thought about it. But . . . look, Nan, this isn't the best way for us to be talking. It's . . ."

"I suppose it isn't," she said when he didn't go on. "I suppose I'm not being very . . . nice."

"Nan, *nice* has nothing to do with it. Oh, all those laws and rules about what you're supposed to think about and what age you have to be to think it, that's a lot of . . . mythology. It's just that talking with you, here, this way . . . Don't you see—it's like nudging a tiger just to see if he'll wake up. We can't afford to nudge tigers."

"Leave them lay?" she said with a tremulous laugh.

"Leave them lay," he told her soberly as they stood and walked out of the dark pavilion.

Chapter 6

Mr. LYNCH had told Aggie Warner to get in any extra help she needed. "With that young man of Margaret's around," he said, "you'll probably need it."

She didn't. Mr. London was one of the neat ones. He'd brought a lot of clothes, but they were carefully put away. And he was a quiet sleeper. Left a bed almost as undisturbed as before he got in it. Clear conscience, all right, Mrs. Warner thought, smoothing the covers, running her dust rag over bureau and table tops. It was very different here than in the city, where an hour after dusting saw every surface filmed again. And very different in this room than in Harry's, just finished. Harry slept like a Mix-Master at top speed, and Aggie sometimes wondered that the sheets and blankets weren't churned to bits rather than merely thrown into tangles in all directions. What restless dreams, what confusing needs, imperfectly understood compulsions, drove Harry through his nights? She took a last look around Richard London's room and went down the hall to see if Margaret was awake yet. People were always worrying about the delicate problems and sensitivity of girls, but it struck Mrs. Warner that boys, because they weren't supposed to have any, probably found their problems even more difficult. Oh, sure, a boy was supposed to worry over making the basket-ball team, and it was becoming in them to worry over school grades. A boy could acceptably go into a decline over not making the right fraternity, over not getting the car of his choice. He was of course expected to recover manfully, quickly, and in silence. But a boy couldn't ache and be comforted because someone he loved had been unkind, because he wanted something —not a car, not center position—something he wasn't even clear about but was sure he'd never have. He couldn't say that he was uncertain, that his desires confused him, some of his dreams frightened him. Couldn't say that he was afraid of being too tall, too short, afraid of not being able, when the time came, to hold a job, of not being able, when the time came, to prove himself immediately a man.

She opened Margaret's door softly. Asleep. Fan of brown hair, curve of cheek, arms beside her head (with fists clenched)—all quite motionless. Mrs. Warner closed the door and went downstairs.

"Want me to stir up Margaret's breakfast?" her husband asked as she entered the kitchen.

"Still asleep."

"Where's Mr. London?"

"He had an early golf date. I fixed him something before you woke up, and Harry was gone before that." Aggie pulled a menu list and a marketing sheet toward her and sat down at the table. She wrote: endive, 1 lb.; tomatoes, 5 lbs.; escarole, 2 heads; 2 lettuce; 3 doz. oranges. She looked up. "I have broiled lobster planned for Friday night. Do you think Mr. Lynch will be back for a seven-thirty dinner? The kids are going to a dance that night, so I wouldn't want to make it much later."

"He said to pick him up right after lunch, so we should be back by four, four-thirty."

Aggie nodded. She wrote: 3 honeydews, 3 cantaloupes. Raspberries, 1 qt. "Do you really think I can trust Harry to do this?" Her husband looked mildly puzzled. "You said that if I asked Harry to do the marketing and pick up the laundry at Mrs. Morrison's, then you could get the downstairs floors waxed today."

"Oh. Well, sure. Why can't he?"

"I'm trying to picture Harry selecting a decent basket of raspberries. He'll take whatever that grocer hands him."

"Probably the Gunning girl will go along with him. She ought to know decent fruit."

"Why?"

"Just strikes me that way. The Gunnings are sort of

old-fashioned, in a way. I'll bet they've taught that girl to cook, even. Should be more girls taught that."

"You mean Margaret?"

"Her and others. Now look, Aggie, this fellow London looks like he means business, and if they do get married it'll come as an awful shock to Margaret that houses don't clean themselves and meals don't cook themselves. I'm sure that's what she thinks now. And even if London is doing pretty well, it won't be the same as she's had before, with you and Nora—and me, too—smoothing the path before her. Do you think the girl's capable of getting a dish of cold cuts and potato salad on the table?"

Mrs. Warner turned her pencil from point end to eraser and back again. She shook her head. "I *tried* now and then. But it wasn't as if her mother wanted her to learn. I honestly don't think Katherine Lynch ever gave a thought in her life to cooking. And then, when she got sick— Well, it was probably too late by then, anyway."

Warner patted his wife's head. "I'm not blaming you, Aggie. Or even poor Mrs. Lynch. She didn't know better, her head was so full of music and books . . . Nobody taught her either. I was only saying that I think the Gunning girl would know a good basket of berries, and I think more girls should. But I'm not *blaming* anybody."

"I wonder what the Gunnings think of this sudden attraction of Harry and Nan's?"

"Sudden?" said Warner. "They've always more or less hung around together."

"Not the way it's been this week. There's something different. Harry's terribly moody."

"Harry's always moody."

"Not like now," she persisted. "I think they're in love with each other."

"So? They'll both be in love plenty of times. Kids get at it earlier these days, that's all. Must say I'd have expected something like this from Harry quite a while ago except, of course, for his mother. I never did think that was healthy."

"She couldn't help it. She loved him, and she was dying."

"Might have given a little more thought to him, just the same. Do you think it was good for him, hanging around that room all the time, listening to music, never getting out with other boys, even? Much less girls."

"You know I didn't think it was good. But what could I say? How do we know what it can be like to be young and lovely, to love your children and your life and be losing them?" She said sadly, "No, I didn't think it was good, and I think Harry will pay, one way or another, all his life for those months. But I can't find it in my heart to say anything against her."

"She may have loved her children," Warner said dryly, "but it was Harry she clamped down on. Margaret came out of it better."

"Don't." Mrs. Warner crosshatched her grocery list. "Perhaps Margaret, just because she wasn't—clamped down on, as you say—came out of it worse. I used to feel that she almost—hated her mother for not wanting her as much as she did Harry."

"*Hated* her? That's the silliest thing I've ever heard you say, Aggie. Why Margaret couldn't hate anything. She's the dearest, sweetest—" He broke off, beyond speech. Margaret was his pet, and he saw in her what she intended not only for him but for the world to see—an easy, affectionate creature, skimming from pleasure to pleasure, leaving behind her only patterns of brightness. "Why, she's one of the gayest, most popular—" Warner began again and once more was rendered speechless at the thought of Margaret's hating anyone. But hating her *mother!* It was shocking, that's what it was. And coming from his own Aggie! "Why she's the most—"

"Warner, dear. I'm sorry," said Aggie, who was herself faintly confounded by what she'd said. "Of course I didn't mean it . . . only that there was something odd . . . Her not going to the funeral—"

"She was sick," Warner explained in a voice that said such a thing should not have needed explanation. "The kid could scarcely lift her head, from crying and . . . Aggie, I don't understand you."

"I guess I don't understand myself. I meant something, but whatever it was has gone, and I didn't say it right. Of course she loved her mother."

White onions, 4 lbs., she wrote. Bunch radishes, bunch watercress . . .

What *had* she meant?

Henry Lynch had been with his wife when she died, and he had had to tell his children, tell the Warners. Though they had known she would die, that the actual moment would come, there had been a draining, panicky sense of irreparability when Henry, walking stiffly, had come into the kitchen to find Aggie. Aggie had said she'd tell Margaret and Harry, but Henry shook his head and turned clumsily to go in search of them. He set in motion, on that day of thin icy drizzle, the strange double wheels of burial. On the one hand the undertaker and his men—kindly, quiet, purposeful, with long and disinterested knowledge. On the other hand Margaret—staring, crumpling, carried delirious to bed, refusing finally to go to the funeral. Sick and shivering, hunched like an animal, she had lain in bed until that clear cold sunny day when they had left her in the charge of a nurse, and Warner had driven Henry, Harry, and Mrs. Warner to the church. Nora was there, and Mrs. Tinker, the cleaning woman. Katherine's two nurses had come. Relatives and friends had come to Katherine's funeral. There were masses of flowers. The minister met the body in its sealed casket and went before it, speaking the ancient words: *I know that my redeemer liveth, and that he shall stand at the latter day upon the earth: And though this body be destroyed, yet shall I see God.* And what help did Harry or Henry take that was offered them? Mrs. Warner wondered, sitting with them in the small room, aware of Henry's wordless suffering, of Harry's jutting jaw and hot tearless eyes. Episcopal in practice; unbelievers, she thought. Her heart had ached for them, knowing they listened without comfort to the words of comfort. Every step of the way Harry had gone with his father, not speaking,

Harry's sound systems—one at the Point and one in his room in New York—were untouched and often blasphemed by other members of the household. Mrs. Warner, who liked a bit of Victor Herbert now and then but did not require the full audio range to enjoy him, suggested that if all the separate parts were enclosed, it would be a simpler task to dust them, but Harry, with camel's-hair brush and great devotion, cleaned each separate part—turntable, amplifier, tuner —once a month. Only the speakers were enclosed, and that, Mrs. Warner thought, seemed to make the music louder. Harry played his records with the volume turned on full, and when he had chosen, as this morning, Moussorgsky, the floors throughout the house vibrated, the walls seemed to swell. Wildly the bells and the tympani rang in honor of Boris, wildly the singing struggle broke on the steps of the Archangel Cathedral . . . *Sláva, sláva, Tsaryú! Sláva, sláva, sláva!* Harry slouched in a chair, eyes unseeing, head a little up, borne on the savage surging song of the procession of Czar Boris in the Moscow Kremlin, in another day, in a world only possible to music . . . *Sláva, sláva i mnógaya léta!*

It had been very early when he'd gotten up that morning. He hadn't slept well. He'd lain all night on the edge of sleep, slipping through, struggling back, but never at peace. At five-thirty he was up, dressed in bathing trunks and a shirt, moving silently through the dawn-dim house. In the kitchen he fixed himself a breakfast of melon, bread, and milk, moving about restlessly as he ate, and then left abruptly—the melon rind, the coated glass, the crumbs, forgotten on the table.

The air in the garden was moist and warm, filled with the chiming single notes and high roulades and thin swift whistles of innumerable birds, unseen but everywhere—far away, suddenly near, just overhead, then past. A daybreak of birds, of wet, thick grass, and the drenched fragrance of midsummer flowers. Beyond, the ocean drummed on the beach, and the harsh gull cries came through the garden chorus in appealing dissonance. Everything awake but the slumbrous human habitations. Nan wouldn't be up yet, he thought, going through the garden, across a corner of meadow, and so to the beach, pale and curved as a quarter-moon, empty save for a pair of bright waterwings that the tide hadn't reached. Harry shed his shirt and walked across the sand to pick up the waterwings, walked back to hang them on the pavilion railing. Then he stood, eyes wandering over the weathered little structure, coming to rest on the bench where he and Nan had sat. Does anyone, he wondered, staring at the bench as if two figures would materialize there if he looked hard enough, ever get over the terrible indifference of *places?* When he walked through the marble lobby of the apartment in the city, he would think how many times his mother had walked there and think how more than strange it was that she should have left no impression, might just as well never have put her foot on that particular rug at all for all the place knew. And now in the morning at close to six o'clock Frank the night man would be yawning, preparing to leave, and the lobby would be deserted—he knew just how it would look—and nothing in its aspect would signify how familiar it was to how many people. For places, for things, we really perish, he thought. You can dust any presence out of a room, fluff the pressed cushions, remove the stubbed cigarettes, and what human impression can outstay the vacuum cleaner? Animals perish, are replaced. Who can tell this year's robin from last year's? Not even the robins, it seems. I wonder if that's what they mean by immortality—to live in the minds of people after you have died? It wouldn't be an immortality through eternity, but I should think it would serve, would do.

He turned away from the pavilion, because it refused to say, even to him alone in the early morning, that he and Nan had actually, in truth, loved and resisted each other within its open aged walls last night. Suddenly he lowered his head a little and ran swiftly down the beach, through the curling water, flattened into a thrusting dive, a long hard crawl. He dived and leaped and dived again, swimming as though he thought of no return. And then in a while returned slowly, at peace with the cold ocean, to lie upon the shore, head on his arms, breathing the sand into little eddies.

She thought she meant it, he told himself. She's ardent and naive. And in love she'd be rather fiercely ready to give. A ripple of pride and alarm ran through him at the thought of Nan's love, and a quickening wish to see her as she wished him to. She would be so beautiful. . . . He rolled to his back and stretched and tried to relax. When she said what she wanted, did she know what she wanted? She was sixteen years old and that was—nubile? But she'd been extraordinarily protected, and would she really know? There was, and he admitted it with an inward smile, a touch of suggestiveness in Nan quite apart from her clear declaration. It was feminine and winning and rather young. Sixteen was barely the end of childhood, and children like to tease. Like to nudge tigers. Nan, perhaps unconsciously, was relying on him to control whatever beast she roused. You'd think it would annoy me, he thought, and all I do is love her more.

He closed his eyes and abruptly fell asleep.

There was something warm and splintery hitting his chest. He opened his eyes narrowly, rather dazed, to find Nan standing over him letting sand run through her fingers upon him. She was laughing.

Harry, with a swift glance along the beach, put up his arms. "Come here," he said and pulled her against him, kissing her, feeling her warm soft breasts on his chest. When they drew apart, he could still feel that pressure against him, and he folded his arms as though to hold it.

He said quietly, "That wasn't very smart, I guess. Sort of took me by surprise."

"There isn't anyone around."

"Always someone around. Some nosybody at a window . . . My intentions were good."

"I knew you'd be down here," she said after a pause.

"Did you? How?"

"I don't know. I woke up and thought, If I go down on the beach, Harry will be there."

"What time is it?"

"Seven-thirty, about."

"Oh. Funny, I thought I'd been asleep for ages."

"Are you tired?"

"Not really. I didn't sleep very well."

"Neither did I," she whispered, and Harry, in alarm, jumped to his feet. There were times when, even if a girl didn't understand it, you simply could not go on talking around the edges of things. The first thing you knew you'd be in the thick of it, no matter what you'd assured yourself beforehand. "Come on, Nan," he said. "Swimming time."

When they were standing in the water, letting the waves curl and rush about their feet, she said, "I forgot what I came down to ask you."

Harry turned to her. "What was that?"

"I thought maybe you'd like to play tennis before it got too hot," she said, and then looked rather surprised when Harry began to laugh. "What's funny?"

"Nothing," he said, laughing still. "Oh, nothing, Nan darling. I'd love to play tennis with you." For the first time since the morning on the beach he felt really relaxed and buoyant, really at ease with Nan. He knew it wouldn't last, couldn't, at this point in their lives, last. But for the moment it was wonderful, like a sudden quiet pool in a river full of rapids and falls. You knew that a short time would take you across this placid surface, hurl you into the leaping turbulence of the current again, and that was the way you wanted it, but this little place, this bit of peace, was so good.

After tennis Nan asked him to lunch. "Come on, Harry. We have loads of food," she said when he shook his head.

"No. Thanks, I'd rather not, Nan. I'll see you afterward."

"But why?"

"I don't know. Don't be cross, I really don't know. I ought to get back and change, for one thing. And Mrs. Warner will probably have some job cooked up for me. She'll raise Cain if I don't turn up to do it. She says I've been ducking lately."

"Well, you're ducking now, all right." He grinned at her but didn't speak. "Okay," she said. "See you later." She swung her racket idly, looking up in his face. Then she smiled. "We're lucky, aren't we, Harry?"

"Luckier than we could dream of."

When he got home he ran up the front stairs, hoping Mrs. Warner wouldn't catch him. In his room he started for the closet, stopped and looked at the clock. Eleven almost. Surely they'd all be up in the house by now. And some music—not a lot, but something loud and stormy, something titanic—was what he wanted. He moved the arm of the turntable across the record to pick up the end of the prologue of *Boris* and slumped in a chair, head back, waiting to be submerged. He hadn't wanted to see Nan's mother, and that was the plain truth of it, but he forgot when the music broke over him.

Margaret pulled a pillow over her head. "That blasted Boris Godunov," she muttered, her nose against the mattress, the pillow doing little to muffle the czar's procession. The boy is crazy. *Boris* in the morning! There was a knock at the door and she sat up scowling. "Come on in," she called. And then, to Mrs. Warner, "Isn't there any way to stop him?"

Aggie shrugged. "It's past eleven. He has from eleven to one, you know. It was a bargain."

"But saints in heaven, *Boris!*"

"Is that what it is?" Aggie said, shutting the door. "I'm going to ask him to run some errands for me, but I thought we could give him a little while. After all," she repeated, "it is his time."

"I must have been out of my mind when I agreed to eleven in the morning. We should have made it afternoon. This is like eating raw meat before your orange juice."

"Do you want breakfast up here?" Mrs. Warner asked. Margaret, suddenly inattentive, didn't seem to hear, and Mrs. Warner repeated her question.

"Oh . . . no thanks, Aggie. I'll get up. Did Richard get off all right?"

"Yes. I fixed him some breakfast. He left before seven."

"Golf, for which no sacrifice is too great."

Aggie smiled a little. "Not everybody clings to sleep like you do." For Margaret an early awakening was like a new emergence from the womb, and she fought as stubbornly as any borning infant. In the days when she'd been going to school, Mrs. Warner had had the task of rousing her and had sometimes thought she wouldn't be surprised to hear from young Margaret the same high cry of resentment that the infant gives when from warmth and darkness he is suddenly thrust upon the cold light. "I can't, Aggie. I won't," the schoolgirl would mutter, burrowing into her pillows, refusing to open her eyes. "Oh, I just can't." Thank heaven, Mrs. Warner thought now, the time for that is past. Margaret wakes in her own time now. Unless, of course, Harry is very punctual about his rights and rouses her with song.

Margaret ran a hand through her rumpled hair and said, "Aggie, sit here beside me, just for a minute?" When Mrs. Warner had lowered her weight to the edge of the bed, the girl, arms wrapped around her knees, head bent forward, said, "What do you think of him, Aggie?"

"Of Mr. London? He's a very pleasant young man."

"But *really*."

"Margaret, I don't know what to say, more than I have. He is pleasant, and kind. He has a very nice way about him. But I guess I don't know him well enough to judge further."

"You're just like everybody else," Margaret said bitterly. "You think he's vapid."

"I didn't say that."

"You thought it."

"No. I did not. He's a difficult man to know because he's . . . always the same. Always lighthearted. He doesn't let you find out what's underneath."

"So everybody decides there's nothing underneath."

140

hadn't known, hadn't been sure, that Margaret knew it. I should have paid more attention, she told herself sternly, unhappily. I should have looked past the surface and found this. Found what? She didn't know, any more than Margaret did. Queerly she heard in her mind the voices of Henry and Katherine Lynch, long ago, saying to a few friends some casual words, not really meant, perhaps, or meant just as pleasantries. "My word," Katherine was saying, "all these *books* on how to bring your children up. I read every published opinion, all contradicting one another of course, and I'm always rearing my children by the book I read last week. Results in a certain amount of confusion, but at least we never get in a rut." And Henry adding, "Well, if there's one thing these psychologists have made clear, it's that children are going to have inhibitions no matter what you do with them, and if that's the case, my children are going to have inhibitions that contribute to my comfort." Repeated, Aggie thought now, such words could sound brutal in their egotism, but they'd only been mildly witty statements, said to amuse. People are always saying, for diversion, without thought, things they would never act upon. Katherine had read those books very earnestly, trying to apply what she thought was good for her children, trying to use her own judgment. And Henry . . . well, there'd been an element of sincerity in what he said, but basically he loved his children. Why did these sentences return to her this morning, here with Margaret? A trick of the mind, she thought impatiently. Only a trick of the mind. Who's to keep children from growing up confused in our time?

"Margaret," she said, "try not to worry and think about yourself so much. You don't have a perfect life, and you know you don't, no matter what you say. But it's a better life than most of us lead, and I guess all you can do is see what's good and—"

"But, Aggie," the girl interrupted, "don't you see that that's just what I've been telling myself over and over? I've counted my blessings up and down and sideways. I go around muttering to myself, You have this, and you have that, and how about *that*, till I'm practically drowned in gifts and goodies. And still," she said in a sinking voice, "I don't really care. Sometimes I think I don't care about anything. It's a funny feeling, Aggie. Awfully funny."

Filled with hurt and a sense of failure, Mrs. Warner took the hand that this time clung tightly. "When did . . . How long has this been going on?"

"I don't even know that," Margaret said quietly. "I think sometimes I've always been this way, and then other times it seems as if only last weekend I'd never known a care." Her eyes were blank, as though she'd retreated from the obligation of sight.

"Don't you think," Mrs. Warner said painfully, "that perhaps . . . perhaps this is just a passing thing? I mean, you aren't always like this . . ." Coward, she told herself. Coward, coward.

Margaret smiled suddenly and patted Mrs. Warner's shoulder. "Move, Aggie, my love. I'm getting up. And, yes, I think you're right probably. I don't often feel like this, really I don't. Most of the time I have lots

143

of fun. And there's the matter of having the most delicate and ladylike of hangovers this morning, which might just possibly have something to do with it. Like the old days, Aggie, when you had to get me up and I never was really awake or alive for ages after you'd got me standing, remember? This is probably another version of that, and I think it was brought on by last night's champagne and this morning's *Boris*. Truly, wouldn't *any* constitution quail?" She wrapped a light robe around her slim figure and headed for the bathroom. "I'm going to take a shower and then if Warner would drive me over to the club, I'll have lunch with Richard. Think he would? Warner?"

Warner's wife nodded, and after Margaret had disappeared and the shower water began to run briskly, she stood in the center of the room, looking at the closed door. How confidently she'd assured herself this morning that boys need comfort but don't get it, that girls need it and do. Margaret couldn't take comfort where none was given. I wanted to help, but I didn't know how, thought Mrs. Warner, clutching one hand with the other and staring at the door. I just didn't know how. She turned and went slowly out of the room, down the hall to Harry, who was not playing his music any longer. He was sitting, when she entered, in his big chair, legs stretched out, studying in a perplexed way the air before him.

But are they all like this? she wondered in the moment before Harry looked up. Are they all—the young—this way? Bright and smooth as enamel, masking heaven knows what dark confusion underneath?

144

"Mrs. Warner," said Harry, rising to his feet, "you just missed the concert."

Henry Lynch cut with care the tip from his excellent cigar, regarded the cigar with dreamy pleasure before conveying it gracefully to his lips, applied a lighter, and exhaled a rich stream of smoke into the air above him. Then he smiled at young Porter in the leather chair opposite and wondered briefly if he would ever see Harry sitting in that chair, prepared to discuss conveyances with respect and intelligence. On the whole, Henry decided, it was better not to plan yet, though they'd have to have a serious talk about the boy's future—possibly some time this fall. Harry might very well make a good corporation counsel (he certainly had a basic understanding of the art of disputation) but had not, to date, shown any particular disposition except a frightful one for running up bills in record stores. Henry liked music and was inclined to indulge Harry in what, as he put it to himself, was at least a harmless pastime. Fairly soon, too soon for comfort, Harry was going to have to make a decision. But now —for this summer—let there be peace, Henry thought, inhaling peace at this moment like the fragrance of his good cigar.

"About the J. P. Wortham matter," he said to young Porter and then paused. "Now isn't it funny how many of these big men have J. P. for initials? Say *J. P.*, and it immediately becomes apparent that you're talking about someone big. Suppose they're all named John Paul?"

"Wortham is James Preston," Porter said.

"So it is. Peculiar thing, though," Henry mused. "J. P. Good as a bearer bond." He smiled again, because everything was going so well and he felt so good. "Well, to get on with it—"

Harry had had lunch and been briefed on the afternoon's expedition. "The laundry first, Harry. Don't forget that. Go first to Mrs. Morrison's and then into town for the marketing. I don't want all that food sitting in the hot sun while you collect the laundry and listen to Mrs. Morrison's prattle."

"Why should I have to listen to her prattle?" Harry asked irritably.

"Because she arranges it that way. The ironing's never *quite* done, so while that daughter of hers finishes the last pieces, Mrs. Morrison gets to somebody's ear. Poor soul."

"Oh, is that it?" Harry said. "I thought it was funny how they were never finished. What do they do, save a few pieces and look out the window to see when you're coming?" Mrs. Warner said that was probably it. "I thought it was the girl," Harry went on. "She hates being a laundress's daughter. I think she hates us too."

"Well—" Mrs. Warner said. Then, not knowing what to say, lifted her shoulders. It was uncomfortable to think that possibly Delia Morrison did hate them. Warner, who picked up the laundry more often than Harry did, had intimated something like that. "She smolders at you," Warner had said. "Ironing away there so carefully, listening to her mother going on and on, never saying a word herself, just—smoldering. Gives me the creeps." But Mrs. Morrison was an expert laundress, and Delia ironed almost as well as her mother did. Aggie had no intention of altering arrangements because a girl resented her lot. Plenty of lots were resented by plenty of people, yet the world's work had to be done, and Aggie felt she already had enough to worry over without adding Delia Morrison to the list.

"Morrisons' first and then town," she repeated.

Margaret, sparkling in white piqué, drifted into the kitchen then, as pretty and composed and carefree as a girl on a magazine cover. "Who's taking me to the club?" she said. "I'm getting dizzy from hunger."

Mrs. Warner poured a glass of milk. "Here, drink this."

"But I don't want that, Aggie. If Warner will drive me over— "

"Drink your milk. I think you should have a piece of toast, too."

"Oh, Aggie." Margaret gulped the milk with a resigned air. "Can't I get a ride? One of these days I'm going to learn how to drive, and then I won't be in this sickening state of dependence all the time."

"Good idea," Harry said. "Only get Richard to teach you." He and Warner had both attempted to give driving lessons to Margaret and had discovered, to their horror, that she had a way of forgetting it was she who had the wheel, and would drive dreamily across the road into opposite lanes, pile gently into the car in front should it stop for a light. It was always gently, because Margaret wouldn't drive fast. "The thing can get out of hand so easily," she'd explained while Warner and Harry exchanged stupefied glances.

"I asked him to," Margaret said now. "Only he won't. He says I wouldn't be safe."

"Astonishing," Harry said. He looked at his sister a moment and added, "You look pretty, Margaret."

"Why, Harry," she said softly with surprise. "How nice." The brother and sister looked at each other for a moment, aware suddenly of how rarely they made personal remarks to each other anymore. How rarely, indeed, they had anything at all to say to one another. We used to be good friends, Margaret thought. I wonder what happened to that.

"I thought," Mrs. Warner was saying, "that since Warner is doing floors for me, Harry could drop you at the club."

"That's fine. Only can't we get going?" Margaret pleaded.

Harry took up the marketing list, shoved it in his pocket. "I'll just give Nan a ring. I thought she could ride along. Keep me company." He went to the phone, pursued by Mrs. Warner's, "Have you got the money?" and Margaret's, "Ask her to hurry, will you?"

In fifteen minutes they had Nan and were on their way. Harry took back roads, where fields on either side were brilliant with flowering weeds. The chrome of the station wagon glared, and everything was, in some peculiar summer way, suspended. Cattle standing as if stunned in their pastures, white and black and

148

yellow butterflies fanning the air with heavy wings, the shrill voices of cicadas going on and on like a mechanism no one knew how to stop. They passed a farmer, stripped to the waist and glistening, perched on his tractor, and did not, as they would have earlier in the season, wave to him or call out a greeting.

They did not speak to one another.

Margaret thought, We are like those dancers—the sad, beautifully dressed, searching dancers of *La Valse*. She could see them, with their gowns gray and crimson, their gloves and glittering jewels, the dark-garbed men with their snowy ties, see them wheeling and running and testing the air with outstretched arms. They danced in the dark—though the stage was dimly alight—and whenever it seemed that now surely they would meet, some wayward gesture at the moment of closeness would take them past each other, unseeing, still searching. A beautiful dance and frightening. Who, she wondered, is the girl in white who will not stop dancing but waltzes on and on until Death himself, sly and handsome, enters the ballroom and tempts her with jet baubles and takes her in his arms? Margaret blinked a little and shook her head. I must be awfully hungry, she thought. And still they swayed in her mind, the dancers who could not meet, and the girl who could not stop dancing.

Nan thought, He wouldn't come into the house. Even if Margaret was in such a hurry, he might have come in just for a moment. What's he afraid of? And what will Mother think? But this is a funny summer, with everything changing. You wouldn't want it not

to change, not to be this way, and yet—and yet—
Once, at the beginning of the season, Harry had said,
"You know, I've decided I don't like realistic art anymore. I only *feel* abstractions." But there isn't any
reality in art, Nan had thought, not answering him because she wanted him quiet in his pose. Even the ones
who look very natural aren't real. Rembrandt, with
his true figures and unnatural lighting . . . But that's
the way life is, she thought now. It looks real, but it's
all lit up in strange ways. She fingered the small drawing pad in her lap, taken because she'd always taken
one on trips to town, and she didn't want her mother
to think anything had changed. Anything? she said to
herself. Everything has, and you couldn't alter that
even if you wanted to.

Harry thought, This is a very handsome station
wagon, and the trio within it has, undeniably, a pros-
perous look. So why aren't things just dandy for the
trio? Cosseted from birth, the three of us. Given the
best-grade nourishment for the body, for the mind,
so how have we a right to feel in any way deprived?
There was something of guilt in Margaret's pensive-
ness, as though she felt unentitled to it, and he knew
that if he spoke a word she would brighten immediately
and answer with the poised gaiety that now seemed always to have been part of her. Yet if he thought back,
not too far back, he could remember a different Margaret. Someone unpredictable, stormy and lighthearted
in sudden turns, but easier to understand than this
unyieldingly happy girl. Why was Margaret so careful
not to be sad? Why did his own moodiness make him

150

so uneasy? And Nan . . . beautiful, teasing, startled Nan sitting here beside him, entwined within him but accusing him in silence of . . . being in love.

"Here we are," he said, and both girls started nervously at his voice. He slowed the station wagon to a halt before the club doors.

Margaret smiled. "Thanks, lambie, you've saved me from certain starvation." She hopped out, closed the door, stood leaning a moment on the window. "It was nice to see you again, Nan, even if we didn't improve the shining moments with any conversation. Anyway, we'll see you Friday. What day is this?"

"Tuesday," Nan said.

"Oh, my word, only that?" Margaret pushed herself away from the door with a light gesture. "I thought it was much later than that. Thursday at least." She waved and went through the door, stopping inside to begin an animated conversation with a girl in an extravagant hat. Harry put the station wagon in gear and drove smoothly away. "What was on that person's head?" he asked, making a wide turn on the gravel drive and returning the way they'd come.

"A hat, silly."

"Oh. I thought one of the waiters had dumped a dessert on her."

"You thought nothing of the kind."

"Well, I might have. It's not impossible." He turned at a crossroads, drove another half mile, turned again, this time into a rutty, dusty, uphill lane threatened with annihilation by bushes and trees on its narrow flanks. In the elbow of a curve he drew to a halt, listened for cars coming either way. There was no sound but the insistent cicadas, a distant mooing, an even more distant bark. Harry turned to Nan and they kissed without a word, remained a long time close in each other's arms, drowsily content. A chipmunk ran across the road, a bluejay came to teeter on a branch almost at their shoulders. Harry turned his head a little and the jay flashed away.

"There's a car coming." He took his arm away reluctantly; the station wagon was once more put in motion. Almost as if we had a pact, he thought, not to speak of anything important. Yet there'd been as much love in that quiet moment as there'd been in last night's tempest of feeling. Not ready for the rapids yet, either of them, and he was glad.

The Morrison place, tiled in some synthetic material designed to resemble yellow brick, stood near the road, ugly and all wrong in this landscape but seemingly unconcerned. An insensitive house, with a parade of iron ducks going across its uncombed lawn, a row of colored stones decorating its driveway, two highly designed wooden tubs, filled with discouraged or plain dead plants, sitting on either side of the entrance. Against the yellow pseudo brick all the woodwork was painted red. It was in some odd way isolated in its clutter, as though the surrounding country, the hills and the trees and the pastures, had withdrawn as far as possible.

In its way, Nan thought, clutching her drawing pad and walking with Harry to the red front door, it's really a feat. Not every house could manage to have absolutely no relation to its setting. Somehow, with a line, with a plant, with an angle of light, the average house would betray the fact that after all it belonged here and not somewhere else altogether. But the Morrisons' was adamant. "Not here," it seemed to say, "and I dare you to guess where." Nan couldn't. In all the years she'd seen the house she'd never been able to place it.

Mrs. Morrison answered their knock, and a smile of pleasure took possession of her shrewd, lined face. Her glance went first to Harry, for Mrs. Morrison made no secret of the fact that for her it was a man's world and a good thing too. "Didn't expect you till much later in the day," she crowed. "Much later. Looked out the window and said, 'Gawd, there's Lynches' station wagon.' Delia's got four shirts left to do, maybe more. Well, it can't be helped. Come in, come in. Sit here with me in the parlor; you can wait till she's done."

"Well," Harry began, "I guess if there's that much we could—"

Mrs. Morrison's small hard hand clamped on his forearm. "Maybe not four. Long's you're here you'd just as well wait. Now your ma's stuff," she said to Nan, pushing them before her into the breathless parlor, "won't be done till tomorrow."

"I didn't expect—"

"Sit, sit," Mrs. Morrison interrupted eagerly, and having maneuvered them into overstuffed chairs, sat facing them with almost uncontrollable triumph. She looked with slightly popping eyes from one face to the other, rolling, with obvious relish, topics of conversation in her mind. She was enjoying this brief preliminary but made it clear that any restless movement on their part would send her plunging into speech. In the dining room beyond them Delia, with her back to the parlor, ironed smoothly. She leaned, as they entered, to put a finished shirt carefully in the wicker basket beside her, then shook out another and without a word or glance for anyone began to press the collar. Delia had a magnificent figure. Nan glanced quickly at Harry, who flushed and looked from Delia to the ceiling to the floor.

Mrs. Morrison smirked and took up a mending basket, drew a breath, and said, "How's all your folks?" This was a mere feint, an opener. She thrust a darning egg in a sock, caught it as it fell through a huge hole in the toe. "Past mending," she said, not listening to Nan's reply that her mother was fine. "Wonder what you do when all the socks are in the ragbag." She rummaged for another sock, this time successfully trapped the egg, and started to work with expert fingers. "Delia was saying only last night that you people"—she indicated Harry—"have from fifteen to twenty pairs of socks in your washing every week. Now, Delia, she hates taking in wash. Thinks she's above it and all." Nan looked at Delia but there was no interruption at all in the flowing motions of the girl at the ironing board. "But I don't mind at all," Mrs. Morrison was going on. "Which of course don't say I'm right and she's wrong. Maybe your pride gets thin, like your blood does, when you get old."

Both Harry and Nan looked at her curiously as she said that. It could have been a sad statement or even, Nan thought, a noble one. Coming from Mrs. Morrison it was just like saying "past mending" of a sock.

As the voice went its unrelenting way Nan glanced about the part of the house that she could see. The hall, the parlor, the dining room. Clean, as they always were, and crammed from wall to wall, ceiling to floor, with furniture, pictures, statuettes, vases, plants, laundry baskets, doilies, candlesticks, magazines. Idly, not because she was interested, but because she was uncomfortable, Nan began to sketch a corner of the room. "Do you mind?" she asked Mrs. Morrison, who tossed a hand in a meaningless gesture and went right on talking. Nan suddenly concentrated, moved her drawing pad to a more comfortable position. She blocked in a pie-crust table, a floor lamp, a spider fern on an iron stand. She wanted to get the spectacular roses of the wallpaper in too.

Mrs. Morrison pretended not to notice what Nan was doing, but Harry bet with himself that Nan wouldn't get out of the place with that picture. It would be propped on the mantel among the other articles of art when they left, or he'd mistaken Mrs. Morrison. "Delia's getting ready to go to the church sociable on Sat'dy night," the laundress was explaining, and Harry glanced skeptically at the figure in the dining room, with its revealing wrap-around and its thick carbon-black hair and slender waist. Strange, strange girl, to be able to stand ten feet from them all and never turn or indicate by any movement that she was aware of them. "They have this sale, see, at the church, all the junk they've been making. Aprons and hot pads and beanbags. And the stuff people get out of their attics, they buy all each other's attic stuff and take it home to put in their own attics and at least nobody gets cheated cuz none of it's any good. The sale's to raise money. For aisle runners or maybe for something else. And then they have the box supper and the dancing. Haven't been to church in years myself. People ask me, I say I belong to the Round Church 'cause the devil can't corner me there." She laughed at this, nodding vigorously. "But Delia dotes on it. For the dancing, to my way of thinking. Just loves to dance, Delia does." Like Margaret, Harry thought. "Course, it takes her three days to get ready so's to be just the thing to knock the boys' eyes out. Dotes on boys, too, she does. But not's much as they dote on her." The mother's voice was complacent. "Reason I'm not working quite's much as usual myself," said Mrs. Morrison, "is on account of this here cyst on my back I had—big as an egg it got before it busted and then there was all this—" She went into clinical and, to Nan and Harry, horrifying detail about the cyst. They sat, helplessly hating her, waiting for release.

Delia put the last shirt in the basket, covered it with a clean dishtowel, and turned. "It's ready," she said, and her low voice silenced her mother's immediately. She ignored her mother and Nan. Fixing her eyes on Harry, who had risen, she said, "You can come and get it if you want." The sentence throbbed in air as though she'd meant something quite different, but she gestured toward the heavy laundry basket and turned and left the room.

Harry gaped after her, went into the dining room for the basket, returned, and said, "Well, I guess we'd better get along. Nan, take that wallet out of my back pocket, will you? How much is it, Mrs. Morrison?"

"Seven-forty. What's that, dearie?" The woman indicated Nan's drawing pad. "You done a little sketch, like?"

Nan nodded, handed the stiff sheet over warily. It was a good sketch, and she wanted it.

"Oh, well now, if that isn't nice of you. A drawring of part of my own house." Mrs. Morrison held it off critically. "Yes, real nice. Even got the wallpaper in right. I've got a fancy for that spider fern, and now to have a drawring of it! Well, I just don't know what to say."

"But I— " Nan began and fell silent. Mrs. Morrison crossed the hazards of her living room to prop the picture on her mantel. "Let's go," Harry said, poking Nan with the laundry basket. Mrs. Morrison, absorbed in contemplation of her new object of art, made no move to detain them.

Harry stowed the basket away in the rear of the station wagon, said, "Too bad, Nan. But she'll get pleasure from it, and that's something, I guess."

As they drove down the hill Nan said, "I don't mind. It just sort of surprised me. How anything in that place *could* surprise me," she added fretfully. "That *girl*. Like a . . . a houri."

Harry grinned and settled back. "Mrs. Warner will be proud of me this day. I have executed the whole thing without a hitch. So far. How about a soda when we get to town?"

Piff's Point fronted on a bay formed by an inlet of the ocean, and its main street ran parallel to the quay. Water Street was short, cobbled. On the ocean side was a stone wall, here and there cut into for stairs that ran down to landing floats, upon which childen were sitting to watch boats and fishermen, or perhaps to watch nothing at all, perhaps just to sit in the sun on a stone wall—an occupation often quite sufficient for children. Across the street were bait stores—Sandworms, 65¢ a dz., Nightcrawlers, 45¢ a dz., Crabs, 80¢ a dz.—with window displays of lead sinkers, bright floats, hooks thin and tiny, coarse and thick, ocean reels, rods of all descriptions. There was a restaurant, gray clapboard and low, with bare wooden tables, where you could get fine seafood dinners if you weren't particular about cleanliness in preparation and where you could rent an outboard motor or a place on a seagoing launch. There was a Chinese laundry, a hotel with a bar—The Farmers Hotel, it was called—and two refreshment stands. Main Street backed on Water and consisted of three blocks of buildings devoted to business. A small bank with window boxes, a fruit-and-vegetable store—LOCAL FARM PRODUCE, its sign insisted, though, as everyone knew, some of the produce was local to Texas or Florida—a delicatessen and grocery, two drugstores, a cleaner and dyer, a movie house boarded up and inoperative for years. Not an attractive town but sufficient for its purpose and obviously content to let it go at that.

Harry and Nan, driving into it fifteen minutes after leaving Mrs. Morrison, regarded the town with affectionate familiarity. Harry parked in front of the fruit-and-vegetable store, hesitated a moment before reaching for the door handle. "Nan," he said, "do you think we'll get like Margaret? I mean, not liking the town anymore and not even much liking the house?"

"Doesn't she?"

"I don't think so. No, I'm sure she doesn't. She wouldn't ever come in here, that's for sure. And she spends all her time at that club. I wouldn't call *it* the Point, would you?" Nan shook her head, and he went on. "A couple of years ago she was just as crazy about the place as we are. Don't you remember how she was always on the beach or the tennis courts, like us? Couldn't wait to get down and cried when we had to go home. But now . . . now I don't believe she'd mind one bit if my father should—" He broke off, stunned. An inadmissible thought had somehow gained admission to his mind. Because if Margaret should marry, and if she and Richard wanted to spend their time, their vacations, somewhere else . . . He leaned his arms on the steering wheel and stared at people going past. *If* that should happen, would his father keep Piff's Prance just because Harry needed it so?

"Harry," Nan said softly, "don't think that."

"Do you know what I'm thinking?"

159

"Yes. But your father wouldn't sell the house. It was your mother's. I mean, it was the place she loved so much—"

"My father is not a sentimental man," Harry said roughly.

"Are you mad at him?" she asked.

Harry smiled a little at that. "That *mad* of yours. It covers everything," he said. "No, I'm not mad at him. But my father and I . . . lately, or maybe all our lives, I don't know, there's been a lack of . . . We don't really get along."

"Harry, everybody feels that way with his parents sometimes. That doesn't mean he'd sell the house to spite you."

"He'd sell the house without thinking of me at all. He'd sell it very practically, no questions asked." Harry wished that he'd never thought of this because he knew what it was going to be like. Even if he and Nan contrived, as they undoubtedly would, to convince him the idea was nonsense, it would remain somewhere in his mind, an uneasiness to trouble and alarm him at unexpected moments. Oh darn, he thought. Why did I have to—

"Besides," Nan interrupted his brooding silence, "if Margaret does get married, she'll probably have children and she'll want to bring them down here and start the whole thing over again. Like when we were kids, don't you think?"

Harry tried to picture Margaret with children and failed. He couldn't even see her married. Not that Margaret was old-maidish. She just did not— Did not what? He wasn't sure what he meant. Perhaps only that she was still pretty young. He'd have said before Richard made his appearance that Margaret would be playing the field for years, running from one guy to the next, having a fine time but essentially running. Richard had brought her down to a walk, all right, but Harry had about concluded that the reason lay in Richard's frictionless personality. He'd be easy to handle, Harry had told himself. Margaret could keep him on the string for years probably. And now? Now he wasn't sure. There seemed to be a streak of firmness somewhere in Richard's easygoing manner, and Margaret showed more and more inclination to lean on it. Harry's mind had moved, as minds will, from its initial thought, but Nan brought him back.

"I just don't see it," she said. "You people have had that house for years, and you have to have somewhere to go in the summer, and so does Margaret, really. What would your father do, build another house? Or start taking everybody on trips? And he brings people down himself once in a while, business people, doesn't he? Well, what would he do with them?"

"You've got something there," Harry admitted. "He sure wouldn't want things changed." He sat a moment longer, then roused himself. "Come on, Nan, let's get that soda and then start poking among the fruits. Do you know when a melon is ripe?"

"I could probably tell."

"Then you're the girl for me."

They got out and walked across the hot tarry street to the nearest drugstore, and later, when the shopping

161

had been accomplished, walked down to Water Street to sit on the stone wall and look at boats while in the station wagon Mrs. Warner's grocery order received the full benefit of the afternoon sun.

> And the afternoon, the evening, sleeps so peacefully!
> Smoothed by long fingers,
> Asleep . . . tired . . . or it malingers,
> Stretched on the floor, here beside you and me.

Margaret, who read no newspapers and few books, did like to read poetry. "Of course I don't understand it all," she'd replied to a question of Richard's. "In fact sometimes I don't understand any of it. But it doesn't seem to matter. I just let it pour over me—like a shower, you know. When you take a shower, all the water doesn't get on you, but some of it does, and it feels good. That's the way I am with poetry, just standing under a shower of words, enjoying the ones that hit me." Richard had thought that was a very cute metaphor. "If I don't mean simile," he said. But poetry he left strictly alone. Read, spoken, or sung, it was just not his dish. "T. S. Eliot may be Mr. Upstairs for you," he said, "but for me—they can keep him in storage."

Margaret had only smiled. It did not require Richard's assistance for her to like poetry, any more than he required hers to enjoy baseball.

Now in the muted evening they sat, Margaret, Richard, Harry, in the seldom-used living room, empty coffee cups beside them. The evening voices of birds were low and intermingled, almost fusing with the grass-hidden industry of crickets, and the air was warm and lavender and moist in the garden, dulcet in the lit room.

Richard had a ball game on, not loud. Every now and then he'd address the television set. "Come on, Pascual, lose this game. You know you can't pitch tonight," he'd mutter, slinging a leg over the arm of his chair. He looked over at Harry once and grinned. "Guy just won't listen to a reasonable opinion."

Harry smiled. "World's full of people like that." He cocked his head. "Struck him out."

"See?" said Richard triumphantly, and fixed his baleful attention on the announcer again.

They'd had dinner together, the three of them. A pleasant dinner, during which they'd spoken easily or easily fallen silent. Harry wondered suddenly if it was only around his father that Richard talked so much. Away from Henry Lynch, Richard was relaxed, and his talk was more interesting. Tonight had been the best evening they'd had in the house since he'd come. Which augurs, Harry thought with increasing surprise, a rather strong personality. To be able to make us all uncomfortable or bring about peace, depending on what sort of mood he's in . . . For Pete's sake, Harry said to himself, studying Richard more closely. The good-looking unmemorable face seemed, when Richard was not aware of scrutiny, firmer than you would have thought, more assembled. I'd have said, Harry reflected, that in repose his face would sort of go to pieces, would collapse, and only be pulled together when Richard found some eye on it. Now it seemed to be the other way around. A sort of disguised and gentle despot? Harry wondered. Is that what Margaret wants? Is that what she's found in him? The thought made him uneasy and brought in its trail other insubstantial worries of the day.

"Look," he'd said to Aggie, after he'd dropped Nan and driven around to his own kitchen door to deliver the bundles. "I don't really like the idea of that woman, that Mrs. Morrison, doing our laundry."

"Oh?" Mrs. Warner had said, looking up from her list, which she'd been checking against his purchases. "You don't?"

"No, I don't."

"That's too bad, Harry."

"Is that all you have to say?"

"I think so. Unless you want to do the wash yourself."

"Aggie, that woman gives me the creeps."

"And her daughter gives Warner the creeps. Well, you and Warner learn how to wash and iron and that'll be a creep less in both your lives."

"Couldn't somebody else do it? I mean, there must be other washerwomen around somewhere."

"Laundresses. Perhaps there are. Tell you what, Harry. You go out and look them up, and then find out if they keep their homes as clean and do their work as expertly and reliably as Mrs. Morrison, and then come back to me and—"

"Okay, Aggie," he interrupted. "Okay, forget I said anything."

"I thought I'd have to," she said, and picked up a package of bacon that folded limply and greasily over her hand. "How long were these groceries sitting in the sun?"

"Huh? Oh, not long, Aggie, not long. We just sort of— "

Mrs. Warner had shaken her head, returned to the list.

The fate of the house nagged at him. The sort of cramped feeling in his stomach that was tension and excitement over Nan was not a worry, or was a worry too beautiful and desirable ever to wish appeased, but it was undeniably and inescapably with him every moment.

"Aren't you going out?" Margaret had asked after dinner and coffee when Harry had showed no signs of moving from his chair. "That is, I thought . . ."

"Nope." Harry shook his head, then looked in confusion at his sister. "I could go upstairs. I mean, I—"

"Don't be an ass, Harry," Margaret had said, making a little face at him. "I was just sort of surprised. You practically never stay home."

He'd subsided, not answering. But presently he would go upstairs. He didn't suppose Margaret and Richard literally wanted the living room to themselves. After all, if they had to be alone there were plenty of ways to manage that, but still, he'd leave in a bit. Go to his room. Or maybe walk over to Sam's. Something. Nan and her mother were visiting friends, paying a call they'd arranged last Sunday. "Isn't it peculiar," Nan had said in the station wagon coming home, "how everything has changed? Sunday I was awfully pleased to be going over there. How was I to know that by Monday I wouldn't . . . wouldn't want to see anyone but you?"

"Do you hear thunder?" Richard spoke, and as he did the white curtains lifted into the room like spinnakers. "Sure enough. A storm's coming." Suddenly fearful for the ball game, Richard leaned forward in his chair, as though that might speed up the inning or delay the rain. "Stay 'way from the stadium, storm," he said threateningly.

The sea wind entered the room, riffled pages of Margaret's book as it lay in her lap. She knew the poem by heart anyway, and the wind coming over the dark tide seemed to drive it in farther. . . .

> Márgarét, are you gríeving
> Over Goldengrove unleaving?
> Leáves, like the things of man, you
> With your fresh thoughts care for, can you?
> Ah! ás the heart grows older
> It will come to such sights colder
> By and by, nor spare a sigh
> Though worlds of wanwood leafmeal lie;
> And yet you wíll weep and know why.
> Now no matter, child, the name:
> Sórrows spríngs áre the same.
> Nor mouth had, no nor mind, expressed
> What heart heard of, ghost guessed:
> It ís the blight man was born for,
> It is Margaret you mourn for.

Margaret you mourn for. No, she never did, she

never even tried to, understand just what they were saying to her, these poets. Yet there was always this sense of having been communicated with, as though birds talked to you, and you had once known the language of birds. With this one, more almost than with any other, she felt so. Perhaps because the child had her own name, but more than that— She was like that child. Burdened with a sense of loss that could not be worded or explained. *What heart heard of, ghost guessed*. Your own mourner. Aggie said this morning, "You think too much about yourself, Margaret." Something like that. But I think that isn't so, Margaret told herself now. I'm thinking about people who think like me, and that's another matter again. All the mixed-up grieving people who don't know what they're grieving over, the unbrave people who don't know what has frightened them. We are not the strong sure ones who build the world and know where they stand in it. We're the atavisms, the first wary, suspicious men, moving forward, perhaps, but always looking over our shoulders, always cowering at some new terror, some new proof of our helplessness.

Margaret put the book aside and looked at Harry, at Richard. Harry looked thoughtful and tense. Richard seemed at the moment to be attempting to put a pox on the pitcher. They had their troubles, both of them. Petty or important, the troubles are with us always. But they, thought Margaret, go at their troubles . . . firmly or furiously or meditatively, or perhaps even uncertainly, but *at* them. I'm forever flying before mine like a hare. I wonder, I really wonder—not in the alarming sense that Aggie seemed to feel when I mentioned it, but so I could get a little peace—whether I shouldn't see a psychiatrist. Someone full of kindness and knowledge who would dredge up—well, heaven knew what. And after it was dredged and lay before you (in her mind it flopped a little and was viscous and covered with mud), what then? How do they deal with the things they drag from your mind? Clean them up? Throw them out? Still that would be the psychiatrist's decision, would it not? Perhaps she could just walk away and never look back, and he could put it in a book or do whatever psychiatrists did do with the things left behind in their offices. I may, she thought. I may. She wondered how she would ask her father for money for such a purpose.

Harry got up and went to the window, saying he supposed he should close it because papers were being blown about. But he made no move to do so. The air was dark now and restless. Thunder rolled heavily down the sky, and lightning lifted across it. Richard turned the television off as the first strings of rain fell through the night.

Chapter 7

NAN HAD HER EASEL set up at the end of the pier and for the first time this summer proposed to do a landscape, with figure, in oils. The smell of the canvas set her humming. The odor of wet black piles, of salt and sun-baked afternoon, filled her with exultance. There was a snowy armada of clouds adrift over slanting blue waves. Oh, what a day, what a day, she crooned to herself, and smiled at her model.

She had Phil Bowles's little brother Hector seated on the pier, his back against a piling, and the sea and the sky were a background for his brown boniness, his fox face.

"Keep away from my paints," she warned as his hand moved out, "or I'll throw you overboard."

Deliberately Hector grabbed a tube and waved it at her, but Nan only said, "Cut it out, Hector," and went on arranging materials. Hector, somewhat disappointed but philosophical, cut it out. Usually Nan would have made quite a to-do about pretending to shove him off the pier, and it would have been fun. But—if she didn't want to, she didn't want to. Hector, who was eight, rarely troubled himself with other people's motives. He closed his eyes and concentrated on being an animal.

"What are you now?" Nan asked.

Hector considered that pretty nice of her, with the mood she was in. Other times she'd fallen in with his games, as he would with hers, but today he'd not have been surprised to have to carry on alone.

"I'm a cat," he replied.

"What kind?"

"Tiger, a nice big tiger alley cat."

"Kindly?"

"Nope. Mean. And fierce and brave and tired from wandering in the moonlight. I'm asleep."

"Where?"

"Oh, on the front stoop. I'm an object of terror to dogs."

"Why do you do this?" Nan said suddenly, and Hector knew from the change in her voice that she spoke to him as himself, not him as a fierce sleeping cat. He chose to interpret otherwise.

"Because dogs are the sworn enemies of cats, and

170

I'm tough enough to frighten them."

"Why do you, Hector?"

He opened his eyes and turned toward her. "Just because, Nan. It's fun, and it fools."

"Fools who?"

"Nobody special. But it makes people wonder. Sometimes it makes my mother cry. I mean, if I won't stop it soon enough."

"Do you want to make her cry?"

Hector shrugged. "I don't care."

"What an odious little character you can be," Nan said. But wasn't it outlandish for a little boy to come right out and say a thing like that. Or, no, it would take a little boy to do it. Girls, most girls, learned to be diplomatic fairly early. Girls learned most things earlier, and diplomacy was both attack and defense for them. But boys, until they got older, were apt to smash at things, saying what they thought. She remembered as a small child being a little awed by the comparative truthfulness of boys. It got them into trouble where a—a sort of maneuvering would have saved them. She glanced at Hector thoughtfully. "Clasp your hands around your knees, will you?" Obediently the brown thin hands seized the brown thin kneecaps. "That's good. Now, turn your head slightly this way." She studied that. "Try looking toward the beach." He did, presenting his full profile. Nan smiled a little because it was one of her favorite profiles. Wistful gray eyes, a delicate fine nose, and as opinionated a jaw as she had ever seen. "That's the one I want. Ten minutes of that. Think you can do it?"

"Guess so. Do I get the giant size?"

"Giant size? Oh, frozen custard. Certainly, if you do two ten-minute poses and don't wiggle too much."

"I'm set." He looked ahead and forgot her.

Hector, Nan thought, sketching long blocking-in strokes, has the same quality Harry has as a model. He gets abstracted, so it takes him longer than most to realize he's uncomfortable. And hadn't Harry been rather like this as a child, outspoken and withdrawn at once, bold and dreamy, delicate and tough? Probably that's why I like Hector, even though I can't stand his brother, she mused, concentrating on the sinewy line from neck to wrist. His skin was almost rust-colored. She hoped she could get that in paint without making him look red rather than tan. She hoped, too, that Hector would continue to show up for his appointments. His appetite for frozen custard was formidable, but his tendency to forget, to wander off on some private errand, was almost as strong. What a strange child, with his animal games, his calm admission that he could make his mother cry. She'd heard that Hector, pretending to be an alligator approaching the river's edge, had once knocked over and smashed an aquarium of rather valuable tropical fish, and that Mr. Bowles had whipped him for it. A shiver traveled her back as she looked at Hector and imagined him being whipped. What would it do to a boy his age, a boy of his character? How could anybody whip a child? People don't remember, she thought. They go all sloppy and sentimental over childhood, but they don't remember the one essential fact of a child's life—his smallness. She'd been lucky herself. Very little advantage had been taken of the difference in size between her and her parents, and yet even in her safety she'd felt at times that the difference was monumental.

Hector began to thrust his chin forward and flex his calf muscles. "Okay," Nan said. "You can rest." He got up and sauntered around to look at her work without comment, and she noticed that there was dust in his hair and even in his ears. "Been playing baseball?" she asked.

"Well, sure," he said with surprise.

"You aren't tired yet, are you?"

"Nope. I get itchy."

"Well, walk around a bit." But instead Hector took an awkward legs-over dive off the side of the pier and came up whooping. The foam shattered and spread around him and he rode the waves and then allowed himself to be lifted and carried to a ladder down the way. He came back along the pier dripping and smiling.

"You should have worn a bathing suit," he informed Nan.

"I wanted to work. If I wore a suit, I wouldn't. I'd be like my models, going overboard on no notice."

"Well, I think it's pretty dumb, painting stuff when you could be swimming."

"We all have our ways of having fun."

"What's Harry's way?"

"Is that supposed to mean something?" Nan asked suspiciously.

Hector said he didn't know whether it did or it

didn't. "Phil says he and Harry are going to have some fun tomorrow night. I heard him telling Sam Morely, because he said Sam could come along too if he wanted to and Sam said, 'To that dive, not on your life.' " Having aroused her interest, Hector said, "Shall I pose now again?" Nan didn't seem to hear him. "Want I should sit for you again now? I got a ball game on pretty soon."

Nan bit her lip, nodded. She'd be darned if she'd give the little devil the satisfaction of questions. The fact that he'd told her this much in that elaborately innocent way proved what she'd suspected anyway. They were talking about her and Harry. Phil and Sam and Susy and all of them, down to the little fellows like this crafty teaser. Oh, well, let them talk. She should care. She lined in a stretch of distant beach and caught, because he was passing, a seagull for her picture. Only she did care. She squinted, trying to see exactly how Hector's fingers were placed in relation to each other. Hands were difficult. And she cared, even more, about this business of Harry and Phil Bowles. He wouldn't, surely he wouldn't, actually go out somewhere with Phil? You couldn't be certain what Phil had in mind when he said "have some fun," but you could be darned sure it was nothing innocent. Harry had never gone out with Phil Bowles in his life, not alone. He accepted Phil as part of the bunch because short of drowning him there was nothing else to do. But to go out with him? Now? when she and Harry would surely want all the time together they could have, because the summer was passing so swiftly, and who could tell what fall might bring? They lived a long way apart in the winter, and even if they managed to meet, it would never be the same as here. Nothing would ever be the same as here, this summer. Did he propose to waste a whole evening of that? She felt squeezed and desolate, stripped of her joy in the afternoon, in the painting, of her pleasure in thinking of the dance tonight. She didn't want to draw Hector anymore. She wished he would go away, taking his clear profile and his sharp tongue with him. He might not know what he was talking about, but he'd destroyed something.

She saw him lift his head a little before she heard hollow footsteps on the pier behind her and turned to see Harry. Harry, she thought, seeing his eyes crinkle and warm as they met hers, Harry, you're so beautiful. He wouldn't want her to say that to him, but he was. People thought, or anyway said, that only women could be beautiful, yet was there a woman anywhere who could match sorrel-colored Harry walking toward her in his old swimming trunks? Everything about you, she told him. In every way. And she knew perfectly well he wasn't going out with Phil Bowles. After a while, she thought, we'll have more faith in each other. . . .

"I called you this morning," she said. "Mrs. Warner said you were busy. I don't think she especially liked to have me call."

"That the way she sounded?" Harry frowned. "Boy, people have a lot of nerve. She had me working for her again. I really believe Aggie is trying to make a responsible character out of me, and all in a few days.

I don't know what's eating her, but it feels like regeneration. Chores. I had a little list. And some of them I missed," he added.

"Won't she notice?"

"You bet your life. But you can't graft a sense of duty onto a guy overnight. I washed the cars and beat it. Hi, Hector. How's the slugger?"

Hector grinned. "Doing pretty good. Where're you and Phil going tomorrow night?"

Harry looked quickly at Nan and fixed a cold eye on Hector. "Nosy, aren't you? We aren't going anywhere. Phil asked me and I said I'd let him know, that's all."

"Oh," said Hector. "Well, I heard him saying to Sam that—"

"You'll hear a lot of things as you go along that aren't necessarily so." He walked over to study Nan's work, apparently forgetting Phil and his plans. "Say, that's pretty good. You've got that snoopy look of his down to a T." He looked, half smiling, at Hector, but the boy was indifferent, studying something over the edge of the pier. "It wasn't anything," Harry went on to Nan. "Phil can't take his father's car, so he wanted me to get ours and go jangling around."

"What dive did Sam mean?" But she didn't really care now. Harry wasn't going. She had known he wouldn't. The day resumed its brilliance, Hector was once again a charmer, and life was piled to toppling with love and wonder.

"Oh, Mills' Corners," Harry said, attempting to sound offhand.

Nan was a little shocked, but she too shrugged the name away. Mills' Corners, run by a Mrs. Feeney, was situated at a crossroads a few miles out of town. It had a murky reputation. Nan had never been inside and knew no one who would admit to having been.

"Phil must be crazy," she said now.

"Doubtless," said Harry. He added, "Your father is home."

Nan stared at him, stunned, and clapped a hand to her mouth. "Oh, Harry," she wailed. "Oh, my goodness, how awful of me! Here"—she began gathering her things together quickly, shoving paints and pencils pell-mell into her box, dropping things—"here, help me, will you? Harry, *please* help. Take the canvas, can't you?"

"Well, sure," Harry said in confusion. He took the canvas from the easel. "What's eating you?"

"I've never not been home when Daddy got here. And here it is the first day of his vacation, and what will he think of me—"

"He'll think you're out painting or swimming. You act as though he'd gotten back from the Crimea or something. He was here last weekend, remember?"

"You don't understand," she said, biting her lip anxiously. "Daddy likes to have me there, just to say hello. He doesn't mind if I go away then. It's a little thing, and I certainly should be able to manage it when it means so much to him."

"You want me anymore?" Hector asked. "I gotta play ball pretty soon."

"No. No, thanks, Hector. Not today. Come tomorrow, will you?" she asked, and thrust a dime at him, not listening for the answer.

"Fifteen," Hector said gently.

"Fifteen *what?*"

"Cents. You said the giant size."

"Oh, for Pete's sake." She pulled another nickel from her shorts pocket. "You'll make your way in the world, all right."

Hector went off, looking as though he pretty much agreed with that, and Nan grabbed the easel and started half running down the pier.

"This is the darndest thing I've ever heard of," Harry protested, catching up with her. "Anyone seeing you would think your father scared you half to death."

"You just don't see," she said again. "In your family people don't bother to—to greet each other or anything. But *we've always* . . . oh, sort of been on hand when someone gets back, or . . . oh, well, we like to greet each other."

"With broken necks?" said Harry. "I mean, that's very nice and all. But is the sky going to fall if you miss out once? This just doesn't sound normal to me, I tell you."

Nan stopped a moment to face him. "What's normal to you, Harry Lynch, and what's normal to us, may be two different things."

He looked away and nodded. "Yup. Guess you're right there."

Her hand was on his arm then. "Harry, darling, try to understand. I wouldn't hurt Daddy for anything in the world, and he will get hurt if he thinks I simply went off and painted and forgot all about today being his first day of vacation. It isn't the not being there; it's what that means, don't you see?"

Harry shook his head. "What does it mean?"

"That I've changed." She sighed and pushed the hand that had held Harry's arm through her hair. "And I have. Only why should Daddy have to know and be hurt?"

"Why should Daddy be hurt if he knows?"

Nan's eyes flickered with impatience. "If you don't know, I can't tell you." They walked on. "Sometimes I think you're a very strange person, Harry. Don't you have any sentiment? Don't you mind when you see how—how brief everything is? My gosh, you grow up with people and care for them and you see that they're getting old, that they'll be left alone, and even if there's nothing you can do about it, at least you can try to keep them from seeing it as long as you can. I honestly believe sometimes that nobody means anything to you." When he remained silent, she said, a little shrilly, "Well, does anyone?"

"I'm not going to answer that."

"Now I've made you mad."

"I don't think you can keep your parents or anybody else from facing the plain fact that you're going to grow older the same as they did. I don't think it's kindness to try. And furthermore, I think you overestimate their age and how lonely they're going to be. How do you know they won't breathe a sigh of relief and think, Well now, here's a little time for ourselves?"

"I just know, that's all. Your—" She broke off. "Mom and Daddy are very devoted to me," she said stiffly.

"So devoted that they want you to be a freak? So devoted that they'd put you under a glass case and fool themselves that everyone was staying young that way? Your father doesn't strike me as a man who's clinging desperately to his youth. And neither does your mother. I think, Nan, that you don't give them credit for plain common sense. That's what I think."

"What you think, of course, being the ultimate ultimatum?"

Harry smiled a little, sobered quickly, and said, "Oh, honey, no. Look, probably I don't understand. You know me . . . I just like to shoot my mouth off and half the time the cartridges are blanks. You just ignore me."

"I can't ignore you," she said. "Nothing you say or do. Maybe that's the trouble. I'm trying to be loyal to two different . . . things."

"Loyalty has nothing to do with it!" Harry exploded suddenly. "You aren't disloyal to your parents because you—because you like me. Or because you grow up. Growing up isn't disloyalty, it's biology, Nan. You've got the thing all mixed up."

"Well, maybe I have." Nan put her hand out, added coolly, "May I have my paints, please?"

Harry studied her with a sort of desperation, and then, in high daylight, with everyone who might chance to look being given an opportunity to see, he leaned forward and kissed her. "There," he said, and

180

handed her the paints. "Your paints. And my love. Anything else you'd like?"

Nan took a tremendous breath. It came with no warning at all, this piercing desire for Harry. Each time she thought it was safely soothed, finally quiescent, it rose within her again like a limber stretching animal whose spring could not be averted or escaped. She looked up at him, her lips parted slightly, the pulse in her throat quite clear to see.

"Nan!" her mother called. "Nan, come along. Daddy's home."

The two young people started suddenly, exchanged one glance of meaning, and went toward the house.

"Will you come in?" Nan asked hurriedly. "You haven't been in the house since— Oh, Daddy! Daddy, darling, hello, how are you, did you think I was a perfect pig not being here when you got home?" She ran into her father's arms as they met on the porch, and Harry, stunned at the utter transformation of her voice and manner, followed slowly up the steps. They were remarkable creatures, girls. He'd seen Margaret do this, alter in the fraction of a moment from a flickering wick to a flamelike strength and brightness. All to deceive—friend or enemy—those she loved, those she disdained. When they wished not to show their feelings, their feelings did not show, and it gave you a peculiar sense of unassurance. He knew what Nan had felt a moment before on the road, and he knew she felt it truly, was puzzled and plagued by it just as he was. But had he seen it in her glance and known it in the quick air between them because she couldn't help it, or because she wanted him to? Aren't they ever afraid of saying something they don't mean with these glances and changes? Afraid of saying more than they mean, or less? And what do you believe at last, watching them drop one mask, pick up another, discard it, reach for another, and all the time saying, *See, this is how I really am. Now you know.*

My mother was not like that, Harry thought. "Hi, Mrs. Gunning," he said, so loudly that they all turned. He laughed uneasily. "Comes from yelling over the waves so much. How are you, sir?" he asked Nan's father, who, with an arm around his daughter, said he was fine.

"I thought," Mr. Gunning went on, "that my chick here had actually forgotten I was coming."

"Heck, no," Harry said. "She almost broke a leg getting here, when I told her you were home." He stopped at the sudden drop in emotional temperature. Nan glared at him, almost, for the moment, as if she really hated him, and Mr. Gunning's arm dropped to his side.

"Well, I'm glad you told her," Mr. Gunning said. He stretched his neck a bit. "Guess I'll wash up." He went into the house, followed by his wife, who hadn't said a word, who had only smiled and then lost her smile.

"What the—" Harry began.

"Oh, you're so smart," Nan whispered. "So darned smart. Or did you do it deliberately?"

"Do what deliberately?" He wanted to shout but forced his voice down.

"You know perfectly well what. Telling my father that you had to tell me he was home, that I didn't remember it myself at all." She looked at him with bitterness and confusion. "You make me tired."

"Well, let me tell you, I'm pretty tired of a few things myself. If you ask me, this sort of stuff is . . . is spiritual blackmail, that's what it is. Does your father spend every waking minute thinking about you? Of course he doesn't. He'd be an awfully sick man if he did. And you'd be a sick girl if you hung on every arrival and departure as if nothing else mattered in the world—"

"Don't you talk about my parents this way," she warned, still in that low voice.

"Nan, I'm not talking about your parents. I'm talking about . . . about everything in general, about all this being a person we've been discussing. I'm trying to tell you—"

"You pick a heck of a time for philosophical discourse, Harry."

Harry, breathing deeply, glanced at the porch door through which the Gunnings had disappeared. "Oh, the hell with it," he said flatly.

"With me, you mean?" She was abruptly dignified, indifferent.

I'd like to shove her off the porch, Harry thought, and the feeling did not surprise him. "Nan—" He paused. "Nan, *could* you be honest with me? Maybe it's a lot to ask, and maybe girls can't be simply . . . frank. But couldn't you try, for me? You know I didn't mean to hell with you, so couldn't you just skip it and

183

not pretend you did?" He saw her waver and pressed on, "Sure, it's fun to play I hurt you, so then you hurt me and then we can have a fine time making it up; but unless you insist, I'd rather not. It's . . . phony."

Again she surprised him. "All right," she said. There wasn't much vigor in her voice. Quite a contrast, Harry thought, to Nan as she had been on the pier not too long ago. But she smiled. "I'll try. For you." Before he could move toward her, she said, "I'll have to go in now, Harry. See you tonight."

"Not till then?"

"No. Guess not. What time are we going?"

"Whenever Margaret says. Nine, nine-thirty, I should think."

"Well, call me. Bye." She was gone. Harry left slowly, lingering down the walk, along the road, past the now crowded pavilion. He went down the beach, across the gray wet stretch of sand that marked a sinking tide, into the gray-blue snow-fringed waves. He swam steadily without looking back.

"Daddy?"

"What is it, pet?"

Her father and mother were sitting in the living room. There among the chintz and wicker they waited, and the moment Nan entered there was a shared sense of climax in the meeting of their three pairs of eyes, in the tones of her father's voice saying, What is it, pet? and meaning, *You have deceived us.*

Nan made a gesture, sat on the hassock in front of him. "Nothing much. It's awfully marvelous to have you here for two whole weeks. I mean, now you won't have to go away Monday or anything, and we can have a wonderful time." Smiling and smiling. "You know something?" she said, jumping up. "You never even turned on the radio. Daddy, what in the world are you thinking of? Home a half an hour and no radio?" She fiddled with the knob, found a dance band, and turned the volume low. "There, that sounds more like it, doesn't it?"

"Sure does," her father said, and he smiled.

And Mrs. Gunning smiled and said, "My goodness, yes."

"I thought," said Mr. Gunning after a pause, "that tonight we might celebrate. I'll take my girls to dinner and a movie. How does that sound? We can get an early start and—" He saw Nan glance toward her mother and stopped talking.

"Nan and Harry are going to a dance over at the country club tonight," Mrs. Gunning said. "They've had it planned for ages."

"Ages?" said Mr. Gunning. "Well, fine. We'll plan to do something another time, Nan. When you aren't too busy." He looked around the room, nodded, and said without expression, "Plenty of time."

Nan took a deep breath. This was awful, really awful. She hadn't thought at all, when Harry asked about tonight's date, that Friday was Daddy's first day of vacation. Even if she had remembered, probably she'd have said Yes to Harry anyway, and somehow that made it—made it— Her throat ached, and despite the radio the house seemed far too silent.

"Oh, come now," her father said with a sudden hearty air. "This won't do at all. Tell me what's been going on this week. Anything interesting? Any bits of gossip?"

Eagerly Nan began to recount small incidents. Mrs. Gunning, listening, thought, What has gone on this week is Harry. But Bert was not going to be told that. He was being told about Hector Bowles as a model, about a trawler that got in trouble on the rocks, about the drawing of Mrs. Morrison's parlor that never got out of Mrs. Morrison's house, about the Jaffe baby who had surprised everybody by standing up in his playpen. "And you know what Mrs. Jaffe did?" Nan said to her father in an astonished tone. "She burst out crying because it meant he was growing up. Now, honestly, Daddy, don't you think that's pretty silly?"

If that isn't a direct warning, Mrs. Gunning thought, I've never heard one. She recognized the technique because it was a thing she did herself. When you didn't want to come right out and say, Here, I think there's something should be brought to your attention, you drew an analogy in an apparently detached situation and hoped your point would be grasped. She glanced at her husband, but he was asking to see the canvas of Hector, and there was no way to tell if he'd absorbed Nan's little lesson or not. So far Harry had not been mentioned again. Certainly no one had said that this was the first day since Monday that he'd set foot in their house, a place he'd been in and out of like a second home for years. He doesn't want to see me, or Bert, she thought. She realized that for the moment

186

the feeling was mutual. It won't last, she assured herself. We're fond of him, and he's always been fond of us. We'll all, even Bert, get used to this—this altered state of affairs. She believed this, and so it was strange to feel tired and annoyed. She listened to Bert and Nan talking cheerfully, avoiding with marvelous dexterity the sad, simple knowledge that none of them would ever be the same again, and felt stiff with fatigue and resentment.

I'm tired of growing up, she thought, and then corrected herself. I'm tired of growing old. But Bert and Nan were playing their roles to perfection, so she'd better get on with hers.

Chapter 8

THERE WERE LIGHTS in the sides of the club pool below the water level. On dance nights they were turned on, so that the great square of water shone in fans of luminous pale green and the underbranches of the nearby evergreens were wanly lit. It was an effective sight seen from the wide veranda, from the windows of the bar or ballroom. Not many people went closer because the subsurface glow attracted insects. They came buzzing, spinning, blundering over the water, and sometimes fell in. Moths fluttered and drowned softly, almost leisurely; flies hissed in hysterical circles, unable to lift clear once they had swooped too low. No, close by it was not total enchantment. The club manager had considered dispensing with the lights altogether, but such a cry of protest went up from members at the suggestion ("It looks pretty, and no one has to get close, after all.") that duly on dance nights the pool was lit, the insects drowned.

The clubhouse itself was adorned and polished, flower-filled, waxed, sparkling with welcome. A five-piece band in white jackets played till one o'clock and could be induced to play longer when the hat was passed. The guests were encouraged to wear dinner clothes, and most did. An exclusive and handsome club, with the right sort of cars parked outside, the right sort of members within. Margaret, arriving with Richard and Nan and her brother, wondered why she ever thought she didn't like the place. Obviously this was all a shallow sort of brilliance, but a club was not a cloister and only a fool would expect it to produce anything but exquisitely contrived superficialities. Getting annoyed with the club for not being something else was like getting annoyed with a canary for not being an eagle. It simply made no sense. Rather pleased with this, she smiled up at Richard, who took her hand and squeezed it slightly.

"Prettiest girl in the Western Hemisphere," he said. "Oh, hello there, Mark. Got our claim staked out?"

"Your table is over here, near the window, Mr. London," said Mark, the assistant manager, leading the way with a graceful flourish. He tucked the "Reserved" card under his arm, held a chair for Margaret, somehow managed to hold Nan's before Harry could, and smiled down at the four of them with brooding approval. "I'll send Tony to you directly."

"No hurry," said Richard.

It could all be done with signs, Nan thought. Never varies at all. But still it was interesting, sort of fun, to come over here once in a while. The pool out there, green and glowing among the dark trees, looked magical, and there was something magical here in the room too. All these floating colors and sounds, the flowers and the ice cubes and the light vague voices, the beautifully shod feet going in patterns over the satiny floor, the air wreathed with music and laughter. She wished that her father and mother had not decided to stay home and go to bed early. If they'd gone out, it would have been easier to forget them for the evening. And she wished, rather, to forget them. This was all very strange . . . this falling in love with Harry, whom she'd liked but had been able to ignore for so long, and this wishing to get away from her parents, whom she'd loved all her life. Nothing had prepared her for it, and she had a fearful sense of being unequal to something now past altering. She couldn't not love Harry, and she and her parents could never go back to last week. Neither could she see how to go on watching her father hurt, her mother resigned, and both of them trying not to show it. Or how to go on coping with her own boldly unleashed feelings about Harry.

And the dance, the party, chattered, moved about, flirted and teased, laughed and possibly sighed a bit. Its voice was many voices, and also tunes and stemware

190

and the sweep of gowns. It was glances exchanged or avoided, recollections and anticipations, sweet, painful.

The party was in the ballroom, in the bar, in the game room. It was at this table for four, where Richard and Margaret were holding hands surreptitiously and Nan and Harry rather obviously were not.

Dancing a little later, with Harry's arms around her and Harry's face and broad young chest close, Nan, her parents forgotten, felt steeped in love and excitement, in unspoken but promising temptations, in a mounting tremulous sensation that the moment she'd been alternately wishing for and dreading was coming steadily toward her and Harry, and that neither one of them, for all their decisions and indecisions, was going to ward it off, was going to want to or be able to. She pressed against him and heard him swallow hard.

Harry turned suddenly, holding her hand, and walked her quickly onto the broad veranda, down its long length.

"Now, sit down," he said, gesturing at the wide stone balustrade. Nan sat. Harry, staring at a black raggedly spreading yew tree, was silent for a while, and then he said, "Are you trying to drive me crazy, Nan?" In the darkness she nodded. "Nan, will you try to think what you're saying, where this is leading? Will you try to understand—" He moved a little away from her and then back.

"You told me this afternoon to be honest with you."

"Honest? But I didn't mean honest about . . . about impossibilities," he said in a rough voice.

Nan stood up and lifted her face to his. "Now you sound like a prig."

"And you sound like a tramp," he said and then pulled her into his arms with a low cry. "I didn't mean that, Nan. I didn't, didn't mean it," he said, kissing her hair, her ear.

"I know," she breathed, and their mouths met and they stood close together. In both their minds was the realization that the impossibility was no longer that. Voices down the porch took them apart, and they sat on the balustrade, their hands locked, reading each other's thoughts. Couples from the ballroom began to stroll out, walking slowly, talking softly. One or two brave ones strayed down to the pool, walked there silhouetted, drifted off again.

"The pool looks so lovely from here," Nan said lazily. "You'd never dream what a trap it is, would you?"

Traps and traps, thought Harry. And some so beautiful.

"Harry?"

"Yes, Nan?"

"We know what we want, don't we? Don't we, Harry?"

His hand tightened on hers, and after a long time he said, "Yes, darling. We know."

Margaret said to Richard when they returned to the table from a dance, "Do you see Harry anywhere?"

"He and Nan went out on the porch a little while ago."

"Oh."

"What do you mean, oh?"

"I don't mean anything."

"Oh."

They smiled at each other, sipped their drinks, and Margaret said, "Maybe I did. Let's scout them up, shall we? There's an—an atmosphere. . . ."

"Yup," said Richard. "There certainly is."

This time they laughed, and then went to bring Harry and Nan back to the decorum of the ballroom.

They'd stayed with Richard and Margaret the rest of the evening, alone only when they danced, and then quite wordless. The party swelled and swayed around them. The party, Nan thought indistinctly, is like a fish with a long tulle tail and glittering scales, swimming about this room so gracefully, eating us up. She felt very peculiar. Hot-skinned, and her head had a way of floating off and back again, fishlike and wavering.

"Nan?" said Margaret, and then, "Nan?" again.

Nan turned slowly. "What is it, Margaret?"

"Are you all right?"

"I'm fine. Why, don't I feel fine? I mean, look?"

"You look a bit feverish."

So they took her home, and she was indeed a bit feverish. Her mother put her to bed and took her temperature, then sat beside her, smoothing back the fair hair.

"Am I sick?" Nan demanded with surprise.

"A slight fever. Perhaps you've been overdoing."

Overdoing Harry? Nan thought. She wondered why she was not ashamed to meet her mother's eye, but she wasn't. Her father stood at the foot of the bed, and she could smile at him easily. And love them both. And not change her mind about Harry and what they meant to do. There must be something wrong with me, she thought, and didn't care about that either.

They kissed her and went to the door. "You'd better stay in bed tomorrow," her mother said.

Oh, but— Nan sank back. It would be all right. There was time. She ran her hands over her body, wondering what it would be like when Harry . . . "Oh, Harry, Harry, I love you so much," she whispered, and fell asleep.

Harry went upstairs directly, and Henry had already retired. Margaret turned to Richard in the hallway and said, "I suppose we could go back to the club. Evening's hardly begun."

"Do you want to?"

"Not especially."

"Let's make ourselves a drink and sit in the living room."

They had only one light on, and they sat on the sofa, Margaret curled at one end, Richard with his legs stretched out at the other. Through the French windows came the endless sound of the surf and the evanescent odor of this week's flowers. Things eternal and things passing, and all for our benefit, thought Margaret.

"I don't suppose you and my father will ever get along," she said suddenly.

"I don't suppose so."

"I wonder why."

Richard shrugged. "Too different maybe. He has an unnerving effect on me . . . like a headmaster I had once. Of course," he added, "men rarely like the guys who love their daughters."

She smiled but shook her head. "Dad's not like that. Not jealous of me. I think he probably only loved one person, really. Oh, he's very fond of me and all that, but not in a way to dislike you."

"In that case," said Richard, laughing, "he dislikes me for myself alone."

"It doesn't bother you?"

"Why should it? It would be simpler if we got along, but since we can't—why that's that. When you think it over, Margaret, it really doesn't matter much whether people like you. I mean, whether a whole lot of people do. It's a good idea to get along with your business associates, and you need a few real friends, but generally speaking the affection of multitudes isn't such an advantage. Seems to me it might even be a disadvantage."

"I don't know," she said doubtfully. "I can't stand people not to like me. Even people I don't care about at all, I want them to like me. I go out of my way, Richard, for it. What an awful thing to know about yourself."

Richard put his glass down and took her hand in his. "Darling, it's because you're so soft and sweet that you're easily hurt. That's not an awful thing to know about yourself."

Not true, not true, Margaret thought with anguish.

There's some reason why I want everyone to like me, but sweetness and softness have nothing to do with it. Why I've—I've *demeaned* myself trying to win approval from total strangers. I've told lies and betrayed friends just to get a moment's closeness with someone I might never see or want to see again. She began to cry. As it had when she was a child, a panic sense of loss rang through her and she was sobbing harshly, leaning against the sofa arm, fists clenched at her cheeks. The gentle kiss came so quickly it surprised her, and she had barely time to fling out, "You don't love me, Richard; you don't, you don't," before she was folded in his arms like a child. Struggling slightly, shaken with tears, she murmured again, "You don't."

"Margaret, I love you. You know that. You're upset and frightened for some reason, but you know I love you." He held her hard, one hand stroking her hair. "Tell me what's wrong, darling. Tell me what it is, and whatever it is, I'll fix it up."

The strength of his arms and the scope of his promise were too great to withstand. Weakly she leaned against him, wearily shook her head. "I don't know. I never know. I get . . . terrified sometimes. But I don't know why or about what. I feel as if— Richard, I feel sometimes as if everything were running away from me, as if I were going to be left standing somewhere all alone, with everything and everybody gone, and just me all alone in some place I don't know—" She swallowed and burrowed against him.

"You'd better marry me," Richard said. She lifted

tear-flushed eyes to his, and he smiled at her. "Will you, Margaret?"

"It's what you want? You're really sure?"

"I've never been surer of anything in my life."

Her voice was spent as she answered, "Well, then, it's what I want too."

A black, late hour. The sky moonless, heavily starred. The revolving pole of the lighthouse beam swung unwatched. Waves heaped themselves and rode to shore, collapsed with a sound of breaking, and turned back to sea. At the club, empty except for those who cleared and swept, the pool was draining. By early morning it would be possible to remove from the bottom the week's accumulation of mud and innumerable tiny deaths.

Chapter 9

Harry came running downstairs on Saturday morning, whistling with exultance. He was hungry as a bear, he was dressed for tennis, he planned to eat everything Aggie could be persuaded to cook, and then he intended to go over to Nan's and roust her out of bed for a game of singles, which he would win. Further than that he did not intend to think.

In the dining room he found his father reading the paper, which was not surprising, and Margaret drinking coffee, which was. "What are you doing up so early?" he asked her.

Margaret looked at him apathetically. "It's nearly

eleven, if you call that early."

"It is?" he said with surprise. "I must have over-slept."

Margaret wasn't interested. She returned to her coffee as he sat down, and her face seemed white and remote. Where had all that gaiety, real or spurious, disappeared to? Harry wondered. For a moment he was concerned, but then his mind turned back to Nan—not that it ever, for a moment, he thought, really turns away—and he looked at the swinging doors expectantly. "Ring the bell, will you, Margaret? I'm starving."

Margaret rang without looking up, and Mr. Lynch lowered his newspaper. "Good morning, Harry," he said pointedly.

"Good morning, Dad. Didn't want to interrupt you in the middle of Reston or Krock or something. Nice day, huh?"

Mr. Lynch smiled. "What puts you in such a fine frame of mind?"

Harry turned his hands out. "Unaccountable, Dad. I'm just—" Aggie came in and he said, "Aggie, could I have a large portion of everything in the kitchen, including a piece of that pie we had last night if there's any left?"

"You certainly may," said Mrs. Warner. "You're certainly hearty this morning."

"Why does it come as such a surprise to everybody when somebody feels good? I just feel good, is all. I'm going to eat, and then I'm going over and get Nan to play tennis, and then I'm going swimming—"

"With the way Nan was feeling last night," Margaret said, "I doubt if she'll be playing tennis today."

"Oh, but— That wasn't anything serious, was it? I thought she was just overtired or something."

"Maybe," Margaret replied. "I just thought I'd mention it."

Harry's good spirits subsided a little, but he rallied. With all these eyes on him, he wasn't giving anything away. "Well, I'll see about it sometime later. Maybe get Sam to play instead. How about it, Aggie? When do I eat?" He fiddled with a spoon, not quite so hungry now, but hungry enough. Funny how he'd taken it for granted that Nan's indisposition last night was purely the result of—what they'd decided. I guess we decided it, he thought, his pulse beginning to pound again even now in the morning before breakfast. He'd felt peculiar himself, and of course a girl would— "Thanks, Aggie. It looks great." A girl would feel it even more. Ah, Nan, Nan, he said in his mind, I can't do this to you. No matter how much we want it . . . "What's that, Dad?"

"I merely asked what was wrong with Nan Gunning," Mr. Lynch told him with an air of having already lost interest.

"I'm not sure. She got dizzy or something, so we came home early."

"I didn't hear anyone come in."

"Sleep of the just," said Harry just as his father added, "I had a difficult week." They looked at each other uncertainly.

Margaret stood up. "Excuse me, will you?" she said,

and walked across the dining room, the living room, through the open French doors to the garden. For a moment as she was framed in the doorway Mr. Lynch felt a sudden sharp unhappiness at her slenderness, her fragility. And yet at other times Margaret seemed merely lithe. Why did she look today as though her bones were thinnest glass, her flesh almost a transparency? If that London has done this, he told himself, I'll—I'll order him out of the house. Where is the fellow, anyway? "Where's London this morning?" he asked.

"Golf, I guess," said Harry.

"Harry, what do you— That is, how does he strike you?" Henry spoke with diffidence but looked directly at his son.

Harry, pleased to have his father consult him this way (when had Henry Lynch ever seriously asked his son's opinion before?) took time to answer. "Strikes me," he said at last, "that Richard's maybe more of . . . more of a person than he seems. I mean, he's got this way of suddenly going quiet on you"—a snort from Henry—"no, honestly, Dad. He goes quiet, and then he looks a heck of a lot solider than you'd ever suspect just listening to him."

"I can't recall ever doing anything *but* listen."

"Well, that's what I'm trying to say. Maybe—maybe around you he's keyed up a bit, you know? Because he's sure enough got a case on Margaret."

"You think—" Henry took a deep breath, confounded at finding himself in such a discussion with Harry but strangely, unexpectedly, comforted. He spared a moment for wonder at this development. Had he, after all, underestimated Harry? A boy of seventeen. But you ran across, now and then (he'd been told you did), children with capabilities, sensibilities, far beyond their ages. Was Harry such a one? It didn't seem feasible. After all, he'd lived with this boy for all those seventeen years and had encountered moodiness, selfishness, unreliability, in addition, of course, to Harry's rather obvious good traits, which included —Henry flailed a little and became angry with himself. Damnation, the boy had many fine qualities. Why was it easier to catalogue the bad? "You think he loves her?" Henry inquired firmly. He'd begun this discussion with Harry and was assuredly not going to insult the boy by simplifying it or substituting patent evasions.

Harry nodded, more and more surprised. "Yes. I'm sure he does."

And now Henry Lynch would have liked to conclude the conversation, and Harry, rather overcome, would have liked to finish his meal and go out. But they remained together as though fixed by the shaft of their minds' sudden meeting. Henry, indicating his newspaper, began to explain his own reasons for disagreeing with the editorials, a columnist, and certain conclusions arrived at by a Western senator. Harry listened with respect, wondering when he'd be able to get away, and Henry spoke with cogency, wondering when he'd be able to stop. Truth informed them that they had had a rare moment of understanding (though no clarity about Richard had resulted), which might only be damaged by further discourse at this time. Inexperience impaled them. Having never gotten so close before, they had literally no idea of how to go about separating. When Mrs. Warner came in to clear the table, they grasped at her as an agency of liberation.

"Ah, Mrs. Warner, would you please tell Warner I'd like to see him for a moment?" said Henry, who had nothing to say to Warner.

And, "Got any jobs for me, Aggie?" said Harry, who could immediately have bitten off his tongue.

"I'll tell him, Mr. Lynch. And no, Harry. It's Saturday. You run along."

The two Lynches parted with alacrity.

Richard was not playing golf. He was on the beach waiting for Margaret. Brown, strong, enormously content, he lay unaware of a group of high school girls showing off for him only a few feet away. He was aware in actuality only of a sweet sensation that was Margaret and an unexpected pleasure in the beach. Wonder why we don't come here once in a while, he asked himself, and closed his eyes, waiting.

When Margaret had come downstairs, Mrs. Warner had given her a note. "From Mr. London," she explained.

"Oh? Where is he?"

"I'm not sure, Margaret. Not golfing, anyway. He had his breakfast and went back upstairs after he wrote that note for you."

Margaret fingered the envelope apprehensively. A note? Why? Why would Richard write to her? She had an abrupt smothering certainty that he'd decided to back out. Well, she shouldn't mind too much, should she? Wasn't that what she planned to do herself? Hadn't she lain awake for hours last night, *knowing* she could never marry Richard or anybody else? So why should she feel stabbed by this, that he'd decided sooner than she had?

"Aren't you going to open it?" said Aggie. The housekeeper did not overlook Margaret's paleness or fail to see the nervous fingers clutching Mr. London's note. Something's happened, Aggie told herself. Something's happened, and I don't know whether to ask, to ignore, to offer any word. They've both, Margaret and Harry, gotten far away from me this summer.

"Margaret, dearest, is anything wrong?" she asked.

"Wrong?" Margaret said thoughtfully. "Why no, Aggie. Why should anything be wrong?" Carelessly she opened the letter, skimmed it, laughed. "He's gone down to the beach. Seems everyone was sleeping too late, and Richard is such an early riser, you know. He's gone down to the beach and wants me to meet him there. And"—lifting her eyes to Aggie's—"he loves me and wants me to marry him."

"Does he say that in the note?" Mrs. Warner asked, taken by surprise.

"Oh, no. He asked me last night. Well, what do you think, Aggie?"

"I can only say that—if you love him, if you're sure it's what you want— Why do you look so sad, Margaret?" she burst out. "You don't look like a girl who's been proposed to by the man she loves."

"But I have been proposed to by the man I love." She looked almost haughty. "Quite definitely."

"Then why—"

Margaret crumpled. Not fainting, not falling. She simply, while standing upright, crumpled before Mrs. Warner's eyes and turned away. Aggie, in a moment, was after her. "Come in here, love," she said, indicating the living room. "Come, and try to tell me if you can. And I'll try to help if I can." They sat together on the sofa where Margaret and Richard had sat the night before, and for a long time there was silence.

"Oh, well," Margaret said at length, leaning her head back. "I suppose I could always get a divorce."

"Now, stop that childishness," Mrs. Warner said brusquely, "and tell me what this is all about."

"What this is all about. Why, it's about love and marriage. Last night when he asked, I said Yes. It—he —seemed—so comforting and—oh, I don't know— beautiful. I thought about how we'd fix a little apartment, and I'd learn to cook maybe, and we'd have fun together . . . But oh, Aggie, I can't, I *can't* live with a man. Share my room with him, my life with him. And I don't know what to do . . . what to do."

Mrs. Warner thought, Well, one thing you shouldn't do, and that's marry. Not while you're like this. If she said it, who knew how Margaret might react? Afraid of so many things, including herself, Margaret had found a rock in Richard London. Protest and cry she might, but it didn't seem that she'd easily give up the support she'd come to lean on there. And if she didn't marry him, would Richard stay around, or would he not? Certainly the situation showed every possibility of getting worse, no matter what was decided.

"Aggie, go away, will you?" the girl said. "I don't mean to be rude. I think if I—if I can be alone for—" She broke off, rubbing her forehead, and Mrs. Warner rose. "Aggie, wait a minute. Am I—am I really as self-absorbed as people sometimes say I am? As Dad and you—" Aggie started to protest. "No, no, you have. You know that. I'm trying to get a straight answer. Please?"

Mrs. Warner hesitated. "All young people are self-absorbed to some extent," she said slowly.

"Oh, *please,* Aggie."

"You seem so sometimes. But you also are capable of love outside yourself, which sort of gives the lie to—to what your father and I have said when we were annoyed perhaps. Some of both, I guess."

"But more of one."

"Possibly," said Mrs. Warner, trying to control her exasperation, since Margaret had rarely exhibited her self-absorption, as she chose to call it, more plainly than she had today. "I'll be starting breakfast now." As she went toward the kitchen Mrs. Warner could not help thinking that young Mr. London was in for a difficult time whether Margaret's ultimate answer was Yes or No.

Margaret scarcely noticed her going. She leaned back, her eyes wandering around the room, resting on a book, a vase, a picture, moving on. I'll tell Richard

I've changed my mind, that's all. Nobody can force me to marry him. So you see, Richard, it simply can't be. Last night I was carried away, but in the end you'll be glad of this, truly Richard, you will, you will be glad of it. Now marry a nice normal girl and leave me in peace, will you, please?

"Margaret, are you coming in for breakfast?" That was her father at the door, holding his newspaper in one hand, summoning her with the other. She followed him into the dining room and during breakfast half attended him and Harry, half contrived speeches for Richard, who was waiting at the beach. At length when it seemed reasonable, she excused herself and walked away, through the living room, the French doors, across the garden and to the beach, where, after a little searching, she found him lazing on the sand.

"Hullo," he said dreamily, looking up at her. "How's my Margaret?"

For a moment she remained standing, then sank beside him, putting her hand on his hair, shaking his head. "Fine," she said. "Just fine."

"Why are you all dressed?" He leaned around on an elbow. "This beach is really marvelous, hon. Go get a suit on, and let's walk way up there"—he waved a hand—"as far as we can go. All right?" She nodded. "Well, go then. Want me to walk back with you?" She shook her head. "Aren't you speaking to me this morning?"

"I had something to say, but it can wait."

Richard, a man without suspicion, said, "We'll have a wonderful life, Margaret. I've been lying here thinking about it, thinking about—"

But she was standing once more. "I'll be back soon," she told him. "You lie here and think about things, and I'll be as fast as I can." The sun was a shattering yellow-blue, the sky infinitely far away, the surf powerful and plumy. Out here it was difficult to recall the things that had worried her in the shadowed living room. But I'll remember later, she thought, and then I can tell him.

It was nearly noon when Harry, having walked the familiar way, turned into the Gunnings' driveway. The garage doors were open, the car was gone, and a peaceful air of desertion held the house. Rockers quite still on the porch, curtains hanging limply at the windows, screen door opening in upon silence . . . Yes, it seemed an empty place, and Harry was about to turn away, disappointed but in a way relieved, as though at an unearned postponement, when the phone began to ring. He had, of course, no thought of answering it but waited in a vague way, as though through courtesy, till it should stop. However, on the third peal it broke off abruptly, and Nan's voice reached him.

"Susy? Oh, how nice of you. . . . But I can't. I'm supposed to be sick or something. . . . Well, no, I'm not. I only—felt funny last night, so Mother says I have to stay in bed today. . . . All right, some other time, then. Bye."

Silence again. In the sunlight Harry could distinguish no form through the screen door. Nor could he hear a sound. Hesitantly he mounted the porch steps, knocked softly on the door. "Nan?" he called softly. "Nan?"

She came out of the kitchen, barefooted, wearing a white toweling robe, a sandwich in her hand. When she saw him, a slow blush mounted her neck and face, and she gestured aimlessly with the sandwich. "Hi, Harry," she said in a strained voice.

"Hello, Nan. Are you—do you feel all right?"

"Oh, yes. I'm all right, really. Mother just—she thinks I should stay in bed today because of— Susy just called. I—" She stopped, staring at him. "Mother and Daddy are shopping. They aren't here."

That never would have kept a door between us in the old days, Harry thought. He said, "Well, maybe I'd better go along."

"No, Harry! I mean, don't be silly. We're— Oh, for heaven's sake, come in." She turned back to the kitchen as he entered, and he followed her there. The other half of her sandwich, a piece of cake and a glass of milk were on the table. Nothing, Harry thought with some amusement, spoils our appetites, at any rate. The *Botticelli* lay beside the milk, opened to "The Annunciation."

"I like that," he said.

"Do you want some?"

"Want some?"

"Cake?"

"I was talking about the picture."

"Oh." After a long moment she said, "So do I." She began to giggle. "Did you ever say when you were little, 'Silence reigned and we all got wet'?" He shook his head, and she stopped laughing. "Just a comment."

"I didn't mean there was anything wrong with it. I just meant I never said it." He continued to look at the picture.

"I got sort of hungry after Mom and Daddy left. So I came downstairs and got myself something to eat. A sandwich and—" She looked around the kitchen. "I guess I'm not hungry anymore, though."

"I'm sorry."

"Why are you sorry?"

"Well, you were hungry till I came, weren't you? And now you're not hungry, so I just said I'm sorry, that's all."

She said, with her head down, not looking at him, "Harry, there's something . . . I have to tell you something— "

"You needn't draw diagrams," he said harshly. "I'd about decided the same thing myself." Only why can't we do it differently? he thought. Why do we have to be stiff and full of unfriendliness this way?

"Don't you see, Harry, it would be a terrible thing for us to do? I *did* mean it last night, Harry. You *know* that I did." When he was silent, she said insistently, "You do know, Harry. So say you do." He nodded. "Is that all?" she demanded. "You haven't anything but a nod for—all that?"

"I don't know what you mean by 'all,' " he cried. "We've said it. We understand what we're talking about, but why do we have to go on talking about it? Why not drop the whole thing? You want it every way, don't you? You want to tease and promise and change your mind and gloat over it anyway and *talk*. . . . I'm tired of talking about it. In fact I'm just plain tired." He was breathing heavily and his voice was raw.

Nan lifted her head and looked at him steadily. Then, without a word, she brushed past him and went up the stairs, leaving him in the kitchen, his breath coming and going in gusts, his thoughts shaken. Once again, without concentration, he stared at the peaceful grace of "The Annunciation." *Peace!* he thought, and went out the back door, slamming it as hard as he could, hitting his heels hard as he walked toward a gap in the hedge. Once there he did not go on but sank to a large stone and sat staring at the grass. It was getting yellowish now, giving up the summer easily, making no fight for it. An ant was staggering along down there with a huge crumb bundle, trying to get around an old dirt-crusted beer-bottle cap. Distantly he could hear the surf and the sound of bathers, and nearer a bird went *tarra-tiddle, tarra-tiddle* in the branches where the leaves were large now and rather tough, wrinkled at the veins. No doubt about it, summer was posting toward its doom, though it was little over half finished. No stamina to summer in these parts. Sighs and goes into a decline at the first sign of age. Very well, autumn would be coming along and autumn had a lot of challenges. School and the rather pressing knowledge that you'd have to make up your mind soon about what you were going to do with your life, how you were going to spend it. To satisfy your father and organize your studies, you'd have to say engineer, doctor, lawyer, whatever. Naturally it would be a profession because—well, because naturally it would. Not a businessman, certainly. Not a butcher or a baker or a composer of symphonies. Teacher, maybe. Is there no place in our society for the man who doesn't want to be anything? No, no honorable place. When they asked him, as they sometimes did, "What do you want to do now that you're next door to grown-up?" all he wanted to answer was, "Listen to music." Well, people have made careers of that. How the devil did they do it? How did you go about becoming a professional listener-to-music, a critic, a commentator, a music taster? Well, he'd speak to someone at school this fall, see if they had any ideas on the subject. Yes, though there were three full weeks of the Point remaining, summer had handed in her notice, and there were all these autumn things to consider. And then Nan would be off there in New Jersey. They'd correspond, maybe. They'd—maybe—have a few dates, have a . . . What have we *done?* he thought. With such a little microscopic length of time to go, we had to go and do this. Clutched with sadness and then with desperation, he jumped and ran back to the house, through the kitchen door, to the foot of the stairs.

"Nan?" he called loudly. "Nan, where are you?" He took the stairs three at a time, not waiting for her answer, and went straight to the door of the room where, as a small boy, he'd occasionally been bored at dolls' tea parties. "Nan, I'm sorry," he said convulsively. "I'm sorry, and I love you."

She was in bed, leaning against the pillows, and she looked up as he spoke with an expression of such transport and relief that Harry, watching her, couldn't speak. "I thought you were gone," she whispered. "I thought you'd really left me."

"Oh, no, Nan. Not ever—"

He took a hesitant step into the room, and she half rose, and then the distance between flashed away and he was on the side of the bed, holding her as though he'd snatched her body from oblivion. It was as if they'd gone up in flame together.

They didn't hear the car come up the driveway. It was only when Mr. Gunning at the front door called, "I'll put these in the kitchen and be right out," that they were conscious of any world but the one that held them alone. The other world crashed against them deafeningly and brought with it terror, a wild impulse to hide, an icy awareness that there was no escape. With a last wrenching glance Harry ran to the door and stood there shaking, attempting to say in schooled tones, "Well, sorry you're sick, Nan. I'll look in some other time." He couldn't get his breath steady.

Nan, struggling to tie her robe tighter around her, pulled the blankets up and snatched a drawing pad and pencil in fingers that trembled. "Thanks for stopping—I . . . Oh, here comes Daddy. Hi, Daddy!" she called imploringly to the heavy feet that came slowly toward them up the stairs.

Harry, white-faced, striving for calm, turned to Mr. Gunning. "Hello, sir," he said. "Just stopped over to see Nan, and found her sick, poor kid. I wanted—that is, Margaret wanted to know how she was, and so I stopped over. Just got here, as a matter of— " He

213

broke off, sickly sure that if he hadn't talked so much or if he had looked less anguished, Mr. Gunning would have let the thing pass. There'd been just a suggestion in the man's manner of assuming that it was natural now, as it had always been, to find Harry Lynch anywhere about the house. Damning himself, Harry saw his nervousness and volubility awaken a troubled gleam in Mr. Gunning's eye, an eye that sharpened and hardened as the two stood facing each other.

"What are you doing up here?" Mr. Gunning said after a prolonged study of the boy's face.

"Well—just as I was saying—"

"I heard what you were saying. I asked what you were doing."

"Daddy," Nan called. "Daddy, come on in." She sounded, incredibly to Harry's ears, as though this were great fun, having everyone together again, as though she'd spent a dull morning and was now delighted to have visitors—first Harry, and now you, Daddy, she seemed to say. "I want you to see my drawing."

"I'll see you in a minute," Mr. Gunning said, lifting his voice slightly, not removing his eyes from Harry's. "How long have you been here?"

"I just—"

"Get out."

"But, Mr. Gunning—"

"I think you understood. Beat it before I throw you down the stairs."

"Daddy! Don't you dare, don't you *dare* to talk to

Harry that way!" Nan was at the door, her robe wrapped around her tightly, her eyes flashing. "You heard Harry say he'd only just—"

"I've heard all I need to hear. And seen all I need, too. You get back in your room. And you start going," he said to Harry.

"You evil-minded old man, I hate you!" Nan screamed. "Harry, don't you pay any attention—"

"He'll pay attention and so will you!" Mr. Gunning roared. "You're both lucky to get off this easy. I ought to horsewhip that—that—" He choked, glaring at them.

"Bert!" said Mrs. Gunning, running up the stairs. "Bert, what's going on? What is this?"

"Mother—" Nan began.

"Ask *them* what's going on. Ask them what this kid is doing in Nan's bedroom, with nobody in the house, and not a thing on her but that bathrobe."

"Oh, *Bert*," Mrs. Gunning whispered. "How *could* you?"

"I can. Take a look at that face!" He pointed a finger at Harry, who stood tight-lipped against the wall, not speaking. "Does that face look like a quiet morning visit to an invalid?"

"Whose face wouldn't be funny, with you screaming and insulting them?" Nan said fiercely, walking closer to her father and staring into his eyes. "Well, *tell me.*"

For a moment Mr. Gunning's hand lifted, fell away at a gasp from his wife, Harry's sudden tension, Nan's involuntary recoil. "Watch how you're talking to me,

215

young lady. I'm your father, and you'll remember it whether you want to or not."

"Bert, have you gone mad?" Mrs. Gunning said. "What in the world is the matter with you?"

"Matter with me? With *me?* What's the matter with you that you allow such goings on? Or do you— " Again he broke off, his mouth open with the strain of huge breaths.

"Harry, you'd better go," Mrs. Gunning said.

"I— Yes, I'm sorry, Mrs.—"

"Get *going!*" Mr. Gunning yelled, and unmistakably started for Harry, who fled down the stairs and out the door.

"I'll never forgive you for this," Nan said. "Never."

"Forgive me? *You'll* never forgive *me?* Why, you ought to be locked in— "

Nan turned, half turned back. "Harry came here to see how I was, and he'd just walked up the stairs and stood there, not two minutes, when you came in, and I think you have a horrible, horrible mind." She went into her room and closed the door, leaving her parents staring at each other in the silent hall.

"Well?" said Mrs. Gunning.

Her husband moved his glance toward the door, back to her. Then he started down the stairs with an air of purpose.

"What are you going to do now?" Mrs. Gunning pleaded, running after him.

"Do? I'm going to phone that—that boy's father and tell him to keep the—to keep him away from here or I'll break every bone in his body."

"Bert, Bert, you can't do that. Haven't you any trust in your own child? What sort of girl do you think Nan is?"

"I saw it in his eyes, I tell you. I could see it in his eyes. Don't you think I know what I'm talking about?"

"No, I don't. And I don't think you think so either. And I'm sick just listening to you."

Mr. Gunning picked up the phone, with a warning glance at his wife, and she, after a desolate gesture which went ignored, hurried away, closing the kitchen door so as not to hear him. She began to store away the groceries, wondering what difference it made if the meat was refrigerated or not. Who would be able to eat around here today? Who'd ever be able to eat in this family again? Absently she studied the piece of cake, the half a sandwich, the glass of milk. So she came down to eat, did she? Mrs. Gunning thought, with a little smile. The smile faded as she continued to look at the snack. Why wasn't it eaten? Why had Nan— Suddenly, with a fearful glance at the door, she threw the sandwich away, dumped the milk down the drain, and pushed the cake into the breadbox. Her eyes felt glazed, almost as if she were going to faint. Oh, Nan, no, she pleaded. Nan, you couldn't have. . . .

When her husband came into the kitchen, she thought the hardest thing she'd ever had to do was simply prepare her glance to be unreadable. She continued to sort and store the groceries with shaking hands, wondering what in the world any of them would do now. It was as if the entire fabric of life had been savagely ripped. You had to try to mend it because it was all the life you had. But how and with what and where did you begin? I hope Mr. Lynch was out, she prayed. I hope Bert couldn't get him and that in a little while he'll hate having tried to. Because she knew Bert. His temper, particularly in matters concerning Nan, was a demon too easily roused, but time could put it down and shame could stun it. Shame, indeed, was always on its heels, crushing them all. She shook her head. Put that way it seemed as though Bert were often this possessed, when in truth there'd been not a half a dozen times in their life together when he'd let that demon loose. The trouble was that the occasions were so memorable. And this one passed all reason. I knew, she told herself bleakly, that he wouldn't relinquish Nan without a struggle. But oh, *why* did Harry have to come this morning? Why did we have to be away or Nan in bed? Why didn't I let her get up when she wasn't very sick and told me so? This might so easily not have happened if only . . . *if only* . . .

Bert pulled out a kitchen chair and sat down heavily. Elbow on the table, he clutched his hair with white-knuckled fingers. He's waiting for me to speak, Mrs. Gunning thought. She had nothing to say.

This misery and disgust and plain fright was a thing that swam around him in a spiraling aura, that pushed within him heavily, hotly, half blinding his vision and causing his feet to stumble. He went past Susy Meyers' greeting without hearing it, pushed past Warner in the garden without seeing him, and started up the stairs with a single compulsion, to get to his room and close the door and stop thinking.

Dimly he heard his name, continued upward, heard it again and turned stupidly to look down and see his father's horrified face. The mouth on the face opened and once again he heard, "Harry!"

It was hard to answer, but he supposed he had, because his father went on. "Harry, come down here." He indicated the study door. "I want to talk to you."

Still he hesitated, not in defiance but simply because he was not sure he *could* go down and be talked to. He had to get to his room, didn't he? And anything his father had to say was nothing he wanted to listen to. There was nothing anyone could say now that would be more than a noise in his ears.

"I'm waiting for you," his father said.

Slowly Harry descended the stairs, followed the slim straight figure into the study, sat down while the door was closed, while his father took up a position leaning on the study desk. *An engineer*, thought Harry, *is commissioned to build a bridge. . . .*

"I just had a phone call from Gunning," Mr. Lynch said. He took off his glasses, blinked, replaced them. "Gunning has a—revolting accusation to make."

Revolting, thought Harry. Not incredible, revolting. Well, there was no reason why his father should term it incredible, since it so very nearly hadn't been. But he would have given much—a very great deal—if his father had said *preposterous*. That's logic for you, Harry told himself. That he and Nan had not done what Mr. Gunning thought—or maybe only thought he thought—they had was maybe due to themselves and maybe to the time the shopping trip had ended, but the fact remained, they had not. My conscience is not clear, Harry told himself now, but at least it isn't open to inspection. Nan had said he'd only just arrived, and that's what he'd say too, and what could any of them do about it? And would it do any good to say You're almost right but you're wrong? It would not.

"Are you going to say anything?" Mr. Lynch asked. Harry shook his head. "Do you know what Gunning is accusing you of?" Harry started to shake his head again, changed his mind. He leaned forward a little. "Yes, I know. I know he's wrong, but how do you convince a man with a mind like that—"

"Just a second, Harry. I'd prefer for you not to start accusations also. You and Nan Gunning were found in what was quite obviously a—an irregular situation. Gunning is that girl's father, and he has a right to try to protect her when he sees what he thinks is—is a dangerous situation." He paused slightly at the repetition, a thing he was not given to, but hurried on before Harry could speak. "You talk a lot about the rights of young people, Harry. But you haven't shown much interest in the responsibilities, have you? If you care for this girl at all, do you think it's right or decent to put her in a situ—in a position that can give rise to talk?"

"What talk?" Harry said loudly. "Who's talking besides that— Okay, okay. But who is? And what Nan and I do is our business—"

"It is not," Henry snapped. "What you and Nan do is the business of your parents quite as much as it is yours. More so, if you can't conduct yourselves with dignity or self-respect—"

"Stop!" Harry shouted, jumping to his feet. "Don't you say that Nan and I—"

"Sit down," said Henry. Harry wavered. "Sit down, I said." Slowly Harry sank back to his chair, and they eyed each other until it became clear that Henry, for the moment, was leading. He resumed more quietly, "I haven't said you *were* anything, either of you. I don't know. All I *do* know is that an embarrassing and ugly light has been thrown on your actions by a man who witnessed them."

"He witnessed me standing in a doorway, with Nan in bed—properly covered, I might add. That's what he witnessed. What he interprets is pretty different, isn't it?"

"It's difficult to judge."

"You mean you think I'm lying?"

"I mean I don't know what to think. I have a daughter myself, so it's not impossible for me to understand what conclusions an alarmed father might jump to. I also have—have had—confidence in you. But how well have you justified that confidence in the past, Harry? I put it to you as a serious question."

Harry's jaw tightened. "I guess you'll have to make up your mind about that. If you think I'm capable of —of seducing a girl—" Henry flinched. "Oh, you don't like direct terms for some people's innuendoes, do you?"

Henry, ignoring the uncivil tone, closed his eyes momentarily. "I don't like anything about this. And as for terms— Well, your values and mine do not seem to correspond."

"The values of different generations never correspond. That's what makes for progress, isn't it?"

"You're pretty good at sophistry, Harry," Mr. Lynch said, and for a brief moment was diverted to a thought of Harry's future. He'd probably make a really good lawyer . . . a trial lawyer. Not an adviser, like me, but a fast talker on his feet, a seizer upon and twister of points, a— He scratched his chin, came back to the present. "Some values never change. They are fundamental expressions of what's best in humanity."

"That *sounds* good."

"Truth always sounds good," Henry said simply. He walked around his desk and sat down. "I suppose a lot of this is my fault."

"A lot of what?" Harry said sullenly.

"A lot of the—difficulty we've had with you since your mother died," Henry said. His face felt stiff as a mask, and the words labored out.

For minutes neither of them spoke again. Minutes filled with their soundless thoughts, with the clean clip of Warner's shears, with the measured message of the big hall clock. Then Harry leaned his head back and said, "Well, anyway, I'm glad she isn't hearing this. I guess she was the bravest person who ever lived. Not afraid to die, not afraid of anything. But this would have been awful for her."

"And why do you say she was not afraid to die?"

Harry looked up. "Because she wasn't. You could tell it in everything she said and did. In *everything*. You didn't understand her very well, did you?"

"I know she was afraid. Bitterly afraid," Henry said in a slow deliberate voice. "Brave enough not to let you and Margaret know, although I've never been sure if that was the right kind of bravery. I thought you'd seen through it—"

Harry sat forward tensely. "There was nothing to see through because it was all straight, all true. What makes you think you know so much more than I do?"

"Because I was with her," Henry said with a sudden hardness against this boy who'd had more of Katherine's love than anyone else had had. "Because I was with her night after night, all night, trying to help her in what way I could. That's how I know."

"But why should she tell you? Why not me? I was with her all the time. I gave up practically everything else in the world to be with her, and I wanted to, so why wouldn't she tell me? I was her son!"

"I was her husband," Henry said. His brief hostility toward Harry subsided. Yes, I was her husband. She gave Harry her love, but she gave me her fear, and who's to say that one trust is greater than the other? "I'm sorry this came up," he said, looking at the boy's hard, shocked, withdrawn face. "I don't know how it did, and I'm sorry. In a way I've perhaps betrayed a trust. But I think it's time you clarify your thinking, Harry. It isn't healthy or good to make a saint of anyone. Love your mother for her humanity, not for a saintliness that she couldn't have."

Don't you tell me how to love my mother, Harry thought, but said nothing. And then he realized that since her death these last few days with Nan had been the first in which he hadn't thought of her. That didn't mean forgetting. It didn't change his love. He looked up to say something to his father, just as Henry said, "You aren't to see Nan Gunning anymore, Harry."

It was like a blow on the back, unexpected and enraging. "Are you crazy?" he exploded.

"I am not. Her father wishes you not to see her, and I wish you not to. Is that clear?"

"Clear? Clear? I don't know what you're talking about. You can both wish yourselves into a coma, but you can't tell Nan and me not to see each other—"

"This may not be permanent. Perhaps next summer—"

"Next summer?" Harry echoed. What did next summer have to do with it? He'd see Nan when he wanted to, and all the fathers in the world couldn't stop them. "No, it's not clear. And I won't obey you." *Why had he used that horrible word?* "I won't pay any attention—"

"You will, because at the first attempt you make to see her, the Gunnings are going back to New Jersey." Harry looked at him blankly, hearing the words and making no sense out of them. "I'd like to say, Harry, that I'm sorry this has happened, sorry you're being hurt. Sorrier than you'll believe, I imagine. But somehow, some way, you've got to be made to recognize your obligations to society. Values—"

"You can take your values and shove them," Harry said coarsely, getting up. "I'll—"

"Go away, Harry."

"No, I won't. I want to tell you—"

"I said, go away. I am ill, looking at you and listening to you. Leave the room, please." His father's eyes were closed again, his mouth drawn with distaste.

"A lot of renunciation for one small vulgarism," Harry said with a trace of alarm that he battled down. "You talk about values—"

"If you won't leave, I'll have to."

Harry stared at the forbidding, shuttered face, then turned and left the study. When he got to his room he was so drenched with perspiration that he shivered in the August heat. Dully he removed his clothes, showered, dressed again. He was filled with a cloudy rebellion, unable to direct it. What did he do now? There seemed, all of a sudden, to be no avenue to follow, no point to aim at. He was boxed all around in darkness. Only you couldn't just stand in darkness forever. You had to make a move, take a step. You had to do *something*. And his father wasn't fair. Hadn't he ever been goaded and driven enough to use some vile term? Didn't using ugly words ever release a tension within him? What kind of man was he that he could sicken so over a stupid piece of vulgarity? So refined, so fastidious, so—bloodless. She wasn't afraid, he told himself suddenly. She pretended to be because *he* was afraid, to help him. He wanted to laugh. He did, softly, and then stopped, recalling his father's voice, his father's steady gray eyes. Henry Lynch would never lie. Oh, the hell with it all, thought Harry. With *all* of it, *all* of you—

"Harry? Harry, there's a phone call for you." Mrs. Warner's voice and knock at the door brought him around staring. "Did you hear me?"

"Yes. All right, Aggie." She sounded perfectly normal. Apparently the scene in the study had not been overheard and was to be kept *in camera*. He tried to smile at her as he walked toward the upstairs phone and perhaps succeeded. In any case she went back downstairs without a word.

It was Phil Bowles asking about Mills' Corners. Most persistent guy that ever lived, Harry thought indifferently, about to refuse. Then, with what he assured himself was brisk decision, he said, "Okay, Phil. I'll get the station wagon and pick you up at your house."

"Are you kidding?" Phil asked incredulously.

"You're pretty hard to satisfy. Yak about this all week and then flutter with surprise when I say Yes."

"Okay, Harry, okay. Don't get excited. You'll be along pretty soon?"

"That's what I said." He hung up and returned to his room. Discarded clothes lay strewn about, something he would not ordinarily have noticed. Now, after a moment's hesitation, he picked them up. Shirt by the window, shorts by the bureau, socks and tennis shoes, finally they were all in his hands and he looked about, wondering what to do with them. "Ah, nuts," he said, and dropping the bundle where he stood, went down the back stairs.

Warner was in the garage, getting out the power mower. He looked up with a smile of great fondness as Harry entered, and the boy stood in the doorway looking at him, forgetful for the moment of his request. There'd been a time when he'd come to Warner with things that seemed past repair, with problems he couldn't solve alone. Long ago, or perhaps not too long ago, but a time beyond recall now. What a strange thing, he thought, that the years come between us and separate us. More than distance, more than death, the minutes and the years push us away from each other. Nan, Nan, he thought passionately, not us. Don't let anything separate us. The thought of her was an ache in his muscles, in his mind, in his heart. The thought of her . . .

"Want something, Harry?" Warner asked.

Want so much, Warner, he thought. So much. He asked for the keys to the station wagon, rather hoped he'd be refused. What did he care about going out with Phil Bowles? But what would he do if he didn't?

"How long do you want it for?" Warner said.

"Oh, I don't know. Couple of hours maybe."

Warner considered. "All right. But it's getting kind of late. You can't have that thing out after dark, you know. Lose your license."

"It's ages till dark. Anyway, Phil Bowles will be with me. He has a license."

"Bowles, eh?" Warner said noncommittally. "Just the same, Harry, you be back before dark."

Harry said nothing as he held out his hand for the keys, and Warner, slowly detaching them from his ring, seemed for a moment about to renege. At length he dropped them in Harry's open palm. "Guess you know what you're doing," he commented.

"Thanks, Warner. Thanks for those very kind words." He got in the station wagon, backed it out of the garage, and headed for Bowles's house. Hector was lying on the grass in front, a baseball hat pulled low over his eyes, tossing a softball gently in the air and catching it. He turned his head a little when Harry drew to a stop. "Changed your mind, huh?" he inquired.

"Yeah. Where's Phil?"

"Inside, slicking up. He's a dope."

How right you are, Harry thought. He studied the slim brown figure, so casually disposed upon the grass, so casually passing judgment on his elders. I wonder when people become artful? Harry thought, bemused. I wonder when you lose that ability to say what you think and become devious in the correct social way? Hector seemed a long way from it now, but he'd arrive. Even ministers, even eccentrics, dilute their honesty, because if they didn't they'd be considered mad. Even his father, who would not lie, knew how to temper his honesty so as not to offend the world's—values.

"Tell me something, Harry," Hector said, with an underlying seriousness in his offhand tone. "Tell me, do you think it's silly to think I might play third base for the Yankees someday?" He continued to toss his ball quietly in the air, but everything about him listened for a reply.

228

Harry, far from wanting to laugh, experienced a stinging wish that took a moment to pass. I'd like to be a kid again, he thought. I really would like to be Hector's age again. The feeling was only a spark and it died, but he wished he hadn't felt it. "Well, Hector," he began, thinking how strangely peaceful it was, after all that had happened today, to sit discussing baseball with this boy, "the way I see it—you're a pretty good ballplayer—"

"Can't pitch for beans. The minute it leaves my hand it's a ball."

"Yeah, but—otherwise, you know. And pitchers aren't everything. Third base is a darned good position. And the way I see it, somebody will have to be playing third base for the Yankees when you're the right age. So why shouldn't it be you?"

Hector sighed. "About the way I see it, too," he mused. "But I just thought I'd ask. Phil says the only way I'll ever get in a ball park is buy a ticket."

Oh, for the love of mud, Harry thought, why I'm going out with that— "But we've already established that he's a dope," he said, and Hector grinned at him.

"Who's a dope?" Phil asked, coming across the lawn, rippling with muscles and anticipation.

"You are," Hector said calmly, and Harry, taken unawares in spite of his former thoughts, couldn't help laughing.

"So long, Hector," he said, getting up.

Hector said, "So long," and continued to toss his ball.

"What was all that about?" Phil asked as the station

wagon pulled away. "All that about me being a dope? I don't think you ought to—"

"What's the idea of telling a kid that crazy about baseball that he won't be able to play? Are you just naturally mean or what?"

"Listen, all that kid knows about baseball you could put in your eye."

"All you know about people you could put under your fingernail."

Phil shrugged. "I got my own ideas about that." They drove in silence for a while, and then he said, "It's too early for Mills' Corners, you know."

"I know."

"Then why'd you decide to come so early?"

"Because if I hadn't, I wouldn't have gotten the station wagon. As it is, they said I had to have it back before dark."

"Oh, hey," Phil began, "what's the use of that? There's no point even going to the place till eight, eight-thirty. Nothing's going on earlier than that."

"Simmer down," Harry said irritably. "I thought we could drive over to one of the towns that has a movie and then have dinner and then go to Mills' Corners." The outline, as he gave it, seemed interminable, and he wondered again what use it was turning to Phil Bowles for any reason. But he was stuck now, and he wouldn't go back. Better Phil and that cryptlike gin mill than home, wondering how to see Nan, looking at his family, trying to figure a way. Maybe later he could figure something. Tonight he only knew he could not stay at Piff's Prance. He'd get home in time for bed, and that was all.

"How're you going to explain when you don't get back before dark?" Phil asked.

"I'll worry about that when the time comes."

Phil looked at him curiously. "You don't seem like a guy who's setting out for an evening of fun."

"Will you dry up?" Harry yelled. "We're doing what you wanted to do, aren't we? Well, leave me alone about how it's being done. It's no skin off your nose anyhow." He slowed at a crossroads, took the right-hand fork. "Sorry. I'm sort of loused up today."

"Sure, sure, Harry. Think nothing of it."

Think only of getting to Mills' Corners, in other words, Harry told himself acidly. Suddenly, after a few revolutions of the wheel, he relaxed. Here he was and here he'd be—with Phil for the whole evening. He might as well stop snarling. Might as well shove aside the thought of explaining at home why he just about stole the station wagon, and forget that father of Nan's, and forget . . . It was just not possible that they could keep Nan and him apart. They couldn't do it, because he and Nan had to be together, the way the two halves of anything had to be together. They couldn't, not one of them, not even Richard and Margaret, who seemed to love each other, know how impossible it was to separate him from Nan after this week. I'll marry her someday, he told himself. And then he was compromising, in his mind, with the great horde of people who were trying to push between them. "Look," he told them, "if you want it that way, we'll never kiss again, never touch again, never— Until we get married we'll sit with a space ten feet wide between us. But I've got to see Nan and Nan must see me. And don't you see that we haven't done, didn't do, what you're all screaming and hiding your eyes against? *We didn't do it.* So now, let us alone, will you? Let us be together the way we were before today, and we'll be good children and obey and pretend that what we want is as naughty as you want us to think it is." I ought to go back, he thought. Right now, I ought to go back and start crawling around apologizing. He winced, remembering Mr. Gunning's voice, his father's disowning face.

They drove through Piff's Point slowly, turned on to Water Street. Harry looked at the wall where he and Nan had sat, and his hands tightened on the wheel as the loneliness for Nan, the missing her, washed against him. Such a little while ago he and Nan had driven in the station wagon and sat here on this wall, looking at the bay, loving each other. Now he had no way of knowing what she was doing. Still in her room? Still there with her bull-furious father standing guard, her bewildered, unhappy mother silently watching? Had she gone out? He wondered, with a catch in his throat, whether, if he'd stayed home, he might have seen her on the beach. His foot reached abruptly for the brake, relaxed, and returned to the accelerator. There wasn't a chance. Not while Mr. Gunning thought Harry was anywhere around. Not a chance. So there was she, only where? And here was he with

Bowles beside him where she had sat, only why? They were out of the Point now, driving along beside the bay toward a bigger town, and at least none of the places where they'd be from now on would remind him of Nan.

They got to Mills' Corners at eight-thirty. The air had freshened, and as they drove the last mile from town to the Corners dusk was drifting through the undergrowth at either side of the road. A breeze, touched with the scent of rockweed, stirred the trees and flowed against their faces. A gentle twilight, musical with birds and peepers, darkening softly. Harry switched on the lights, went around a bend.

Mills' Corners, luridly aglow, spilling music through every window, sprang at them like a figure from a jack-in-the-box. Beer signs seemed to giggle with color, and sounds of hilarity struck them while they were still across the road with the motor running. The sound of laughter and dancing and high-pitched conversation, a sound quite similar to, just louder than, that of the country club on dance nights.

Inside they found a booth with a table still beer-ringed and ash-littered. "Think anyone's sitting here?" Harry said.

"Who cares?" Phil slid across a seat. "If they are, we'll move." He looked about the room, through the smoke, through the dancing bodies—some clinging as though tranced, some cavorting like toys, some shuffling uncertainly on the fringes. The twist, the frug, and the old-fashioned grapple. He lifted himself a

233

little in his seat, peered, and signaled a waitress, who flipped a finger at him and came in a hip-slinging walk to their table.

"Well, *hello,*" she said. Her red mouth remained open, slightly smiling, as she looked at the two of them, slowly moving her dark thick-lidded eyes from one to the other. She seemed whiter of face, blacker of hair, deeper of breast than she had in the Morrison dining room. She hovered over them, muskily perfumed, in a dress deeply cut at the bodice. The dress was red, caught up at the hem to display a snowy ruffled petticoat. She had a red flower in the pitchy thickness of her hair.

Phil swallowed loudly and said, "Hi, Delia. Didn't expect to find you here."

"You didn't?" she said lazily. "Not surprising. I just sort of got the job this week. Trying it out, like." Phil was looking her up and down with avid deliberation, and she stood, enjoying his scrutiny, assisting it by running her hands down her hips. "New dress," she said. "How do I look?"

Like the Daughter of the Regiment, Harry thought. "*Man!*" said Phil.

"Cat got your tongue?" she said, transferring her attention to Harry. She seemed quite oblivious of patrons at other tables trying to get her eye.

"I thought," Harry said, "that you were going to a church sociable tonight." What a fool thing to say.

"Oh? You were thinking about me, were you?" She didn't give him time to protest, even if he'd considered it. "Well, it's a funny thing, but Ma thinks I'm

234

at that very same sociable."

"What'll she say when she finds you aren't?"

"Nothing. I do what I want." Her eyes moved slowly from one boy to the other. "I like it better here. It's livelier. And we get to dance with the customers. Interested?"

"Natch," Phil croaked. "Put me down for that." Harry said nothing.

"Like to order?" Delia asked after a pause. She didn't seem discommoded by Harry's silence.

"Beer," said Phil. "Nice cold bottle of beer."

Harry hesitated. "Coke," he said. Delia lifted an eyebrow, Phil snorted slightly. "Anything to say?" Harry asked Phil narrowly.

"Your poison." Phil shrugged, looking after Delia, who had swung away and was taking an order at the next table, being rather obviously haughty with the group of boys there. She's pitched on us, Harry thought, and wants to make it clear. His stomach was beginning to feel unpleasant, and the thought of explaining his long absence when he got home was more and more agonizing. What could he say? If he phoned now, would it do any good? He was sickly sure that nothing now would do any good. Maybe if he hadn't beat it like a near thief, they'd have reconsidered about Nan. If he'd humbled himself and made promises . . . I ought to get up and leave now, he thought. But inertia and the idea of trying to drag Phil away were overpowering. He couldn't very well just walk out on Phil, could he? He supposed he could. He'd piled one mistake on top of another all day. Social usage shouldn't prove a barrier now. Still he sat unmoving, looking at the dancers, looking at the other tables. In a corner by himself old Gregg Depew, the stationmaster, was sprawled over a glass of whisky. Harry half rose, thinking he could at least spend a few minutes with a friend of another day. Maybe it would give him a glow of fellowship and humanity to sit with Gregg and let him talk. Especially since he didn't want to.

"Where're you going?" Phil asked.

Harry gestured in Gregg's direction. "Thought I'd talk to old Depew for a few minutes. He looks sort of sad." Gregg did seem to be taking his pleasure morosely, staring at his glass, suddenly downing it with a grimace, returning to a study of its emptiness.

"Sad?" Phil said. "The guy's sloshed. Look at him. He couldn't talk to you if his life depended on it." They saw Gregg's flaccid arm wave at a passing waitress, indicate with broad uncertainty his wish for another drink.

"They shouldn't give him one," Harry protested.

"Forget it, Harry. Feeney's running this dump, not you. They know when to stop a guy's drinks."

"If he's not dead, he's servable?"

"What d'you care?" Phil broke off with a glittering smile for Delia. "How's for that dance now, honey?" he said when she'd put their glasses down.

"Okay," said Delia with a glance at Harry.

Phil got up and almost snatched her. "I'm the one that asked, not Blue Boy there." He drove her off with a muscular rhythm, holding her as tight as he could

236

and still breathe. Someone turned the juke box louder, and with that the voices became more strident, the sound of the bar trade more piercing, and even the smoke seemed to thicken. Harry looked for Gregg but saw no sign of him. He saw Mrs. Feeney, baubled all over with bracelets and earrings and a sequined stole. She sat at the cashier's booth, keeping a hard bright eye on her bartenders, her waitresses, her clientele. Now and then when spoken to, a smile so phony it made Harry hunch tracked across her face and disappeared as if dropped off a cliff. Her narrow fingers shuffled money ceaselessly. In her whole person only those fingers seemed sentient as they fondled and sorted and caressed the take.

Harry took a swallow of his coke, found it warm and thought, Tomorrow at this time has got to come, but what will it be like then? What will have been said or decided? How will we be seeing things tomorrow at this time? How, even though it had to, would tomorrow at this time ever be?

After a while Phil and Delia returned, and Harry, looking up to ask Phil if they could possibly leave now, met Delia's eyes. "Well?" she said. "How about it, Harry, boy, do I get a dance?" She spoke with a lush confidence that made Phil's eyes glow, that Harry found quite unjustified. Without a word, with barely perceptible impoliteness, Harry rose and put his arms lightly about her, steered her away.

"Funny," she said, putting her head back a little, letting her dark eyes wander over his face as though it was a treasured sight, "funny to be finally dancing with you." Oh, yeah? Harry thought. "I mean—" She moved close. "It's something I've thought of . . . so many times. Like the other day when you were at the house, didn't you sort of *feel* what I was thinking?" Her voice was throatier than usual and she felt like a velvet cushion filled with down, a cushion soaked in a sweet choking perfume. Harry lifted his chin and tried to push her off.

"What's the matter, Hawwy?" she whispered.

At least, thought Harry, stupefied, it *sounded* like Hawwy. She's crazy, he told himself, disliking her more and more. What did you do with people like this? Again he attempted to push her away slightly.

"You're a funny boy," she drawled. "Not at all like the others."

"I think," he said painfully, "that someone over there is trying to call you. To order something."

"Let'm wait," she said indifferently. "You don't want me to leave, do you?"

"As a matter of fact," he burst out, "I wouldn't mind at all." He tried to think of something softening to add, then let it stand. They'd hesitated, midcenter of the dance floor, while she looked up at him, outraged, spiteful.

"Oh, you wouldn't?" she said, forcing the words between her teeth. *"You wouldn't!* You stuck-up jerk, you!" A pain crashed against his leg, and she walked away, leaving him gasping before the amused, curious regard of surrounding couples. Limping slightly, he returned to the table and sat down.

"Something wrong?" said Phil, his eyes searching the room for Delia.

"She kicked me in the shin," Harry said, still not quite able to believe it.

"Huh?" Phil burst into uproarious laughter. "Well, Harry, my boy, I'd never have thought it of you. Not in a million years. Old Harry, the bluestocking, making passes—"

"I've had enough of this, Phil. Let's go."

"Go? Just because you got your ears knocked back? Don't give up so easy, man."

"Will you cut the clowning? I'm fed up, I tell you. We've had a hot-diggety time all day, *so let's go.*"

"No. I like it here. Like it just fine. I—"

"Listen, Phil, I tell you I want to leave and I mean it."

"Well—" Phil waved a hand and said scornfully, "Go on. I'm not stopping you."

Harry took a deep breath. "You know I'm not supposed to drive after dark. How much do you want, for Pete's sake? You've had—"

"Stop telling me what I've had, sonny. You bore me. So careful, so good, so trustworthy—"

Harry walked away, Phil's laughter following him. "Drive about ten miles an hour, boy scout, and you ought to be all right."

"Hey, you," bawled Mrs. Feeney. "You there, going out the door! Have you paid?"

"I sure have," Harry said, and escaped into the comparatively fresh air of the parking lot, so much fuller now that it took him a little while to find the station wagon. When he did, when he had the lights on and had run the motor slightly, he began to back up and then heard a scream of "Look out! Oh, God, *look out!*" He felt a sickening sensation of softness and crushing as the station wagon backed up, as, in a volcano of terror, he jerked it forward again; and the voice went on yelling, "Look out . . . look out! STOP!"

Chapter 10

THERE HAD NOT BEEN, during the entire day, Margaret thought, a time when she could have told Richard that his plans were outlines for nothing. How did you tell a man whom you loved, who loved you, who lay on the sand building sturdy, shining castles, that you could not share them? If he had mentioned marriage again—but he hadn't. Because he'd sensed her withdrawal? Not, in any case, because he'd changed his mind. A man like Richard didn't decide overnight that what he wanted yesterday he doesn't want today.

So she had let the morning pass. And the afternoon. They'd gone briefly to the club. Now at home they sat with Henry, having cocktails, and the strain in the room for once did not seem to relate to Richard's presence. Which, she found, was odd. Certainly Richard was talking no more seriously or deeply than he ever did around Henry, the only man who seemed able to upset his poise. But her father seemed not really to notice either of them. He drank his Scotch moodily, his chin down. Margaret noticed, for the first time, that he was beginning to show signs of age. Dad, she mourned with unexpected tenderness, Dad, we don't think about you much, do we, or give you much. When had she last wondered how her father spent his time, what his life now meant to him, whether the Yale Club on Wednesday night was not funny or annoying, as it varyingly struck her and Harry, but possibly the lonely habit of a man who had only habits left to go by?

"Is something wrong, Dad?" she asked him gently, interrupting Richard.

Richard fell silent and Henry, after a moment, turned to his daughter. He rubbed his chin, shook his head, then nodded. "Just wondering where Harry is. He's been gone all afternoon."

"Harry?" Margaret said, mildly surprised. "Oh, he's around, I guess. He's often gone all afternoon. All day, sometimes."

"Yes, but—" Henry sighed, straightened in his chair. "Fix me another, will you, Maggie?" he asked, holding out his glass. He didn't notice the name he'd used, but Margaret did. It disturbed her. It was too much a sign of affection, a term he hadn't used in years and would certainly not have been expected to use in front of Richard, who always got his most rigid aspect. She prepared his drink, stood before him a moment, hoping he'd say something, and then resumed her seat, feeling strangely chilled. There was something more in this concern for Harry than the simple fact of an afternoon's absence.

"Mr. Lynch," said Richard, leaning forward in the long pause that followed, "Mr. Lynch, I wonder if I might speak to you alone sometime this evening?"

Henry, as if half aroused, looked from Richard to Margaret, who'd become abruptly tense and pale. He shifted his glance back to the man with an effort. "All right. I mean, that'll be fine. After dinner?"

Richard nodded. "After dinner."

And now no one spoke until Warner announced that dinner was ready. Henry slammed his glass down, got to his feet, and said angrily, "Where's Harry, Warner? Does he make a practice of not appearing for meals?"

"Why, he took the station wagon a while back," Warner said uncomfortably. "Said he'd have it back before dark."

"Before dark? What about his dinner?"

Warner moved his hands out while Margaret and Richard sat like an audience watching a play.

"Where did he go?" Henry demanded.

"I don't know, Mr. Lynch. I don't question Harry much. He's pretty reliable."

"*Reliable?* I'd rather rely on a leaky boat in the middle of the Atlantic!" Henry strode out of the room, down the hall to the kitchen. "Where's Harry?" he yelled at Mrs. Warner, who was shaking lettuce in a wire basket over the sink. "Does anybody around here keep track of my children?"

Mrs. Warner put the basket down. "It's difficult to keep track of young people, when they aren't really children," she began.

"Spare me the homilies, Mrs. Warner," Henry said. "Will somebody give me a straight answer?" He turned as Warner joined them. "Do you or do you not know where Harry has gone?"

Warner replied stiffly, "All I know is, he took the station wagon and said he'd have it back, as he has done on many occasions. *Always* getting it back."

"Always getting it back after dinner? Did he tell you he wouldn't be here for dinner?" he demanded of Mrs. Warner. She shook her head slowly. "Well, does anybody know *anything?*"

"I know that this seems a lot of fuss over merely being late for dinner. People have been late for dinner before and the world's still turning," Mrs. Warner said. Henry's temper visibly bounded, but she continued. "Phil Bowles phoned here this afternoon, and Harry took the call, so he might be with him. But where, I don't know."

Henry relaxed a little. "Phil's all right. A good lad. I imagine they should—"

"That's it," Warner interrupted. "I'd forgotten, but he did say he was going to be with Bowles. He said," Warner went on more slowly, "that if it should get dark, Bowles could drive."

"Oh, he did, did he?" Henry was aroused again.

"What's going on around here. Do people simply go off without a word, not letting anyone know when they'll be—" Suddenly he turned away with a wave of his hand. "Serve dinner, please, Warner. We won't wait for Harry."

When he'd gone, Aggie and her husband eyed each other. "I think they had a quarrel this afternoon," Aggie said. "I heard something going on in the study, and then Harry came out of his room when I called him, looking like a thundercloud. I do hope," she added, handing Warner a platter of chicken salad, "that he doesn't stay out too long."

Warner lingered a moment. "He looked funny to me, too, in the garage. Sort of—" Shaking his head, he went through the swinging door to the dining room. Aggie put vegetables in serving dishes, covered the rolls with a napkin, waited for Warner's return. She felt unaccountably despondent. Not at Harry's absence, she assured herself. That was nothing too alarming. But Mr. Lynch's strange concern, his nervous questions, had upset her. And she did not share his confidence in Phil Bowles. Henry hadn't troubled to look much beneath the surface there. A gloss of good humor and high spirits, and Henry called him "a good lad." I think he's a sneak, Mrs. Warner told herself, scowling at the asparagus. Each time Warner returned she questioned him with her eyes.

"Nothing," he said. "Not eating much. Mr. Lynch hasn't said two words. Margaret looks sick, and Mr. London's the only one talking. He's doing a good job, though."

"Well, thank heaven for Mr. London," Aggie said tartly.

By unspoken agreement the after-dinner appointment between Richard and Mr. Lynch was postponed. Margaret, serving coffee with unsteady hands, wondered if she were relieved and couldn't feel it or just didn't feel anything. Sometime tonight she would have to tell Richard that speaking to her father was no longer necessary, that no trips would have to be planned, no furniture purchased, no castles constructed. Only now, for just this time, it seemed enough to have Richard quietly commenting on quiet subjects, to have Richard not allowing the perilous silence to fall. A silence that seemed to hover above their heads, ready to pounce and fix them fearfully until Harry should return.

But where could he be, and how could he do this to them? And why didn't he call or let them know or do anything at all to lift this queer unrealizable threat from their minds? Why, most of all, had the threat taken such shape? Surely a boy of seventeen now and then did thoughtless things (Harry often did) without plunging everyone into unquiet misgivings? He was late; he was inconsiderate. Why were they all waiting like this for something more, something awful, to come of it? Dad's done this, she thought. He's injected us with some apprehension of his own. Even when Harry ran away last week, it wasn't like this. There's something more. Something has happened, and he won't tell us what it is.

She shivered uncontrollably. Richard, beside her, put a warm firm hand on hers. She pulled away. Oh, don't, Richard, she told him, but could not meet his eyes. Don't, because I'm going to hurt you very soon, and you only make it harder. It was strange and stupid that now, when she'd decided to refuse Richard, her father should seem for the first time rather to welcome him. Richard's helping him, she thought. Perhaps only keeping his own thoughts away but helping him.

"And so," Richard was saying, "you have to admit that whether or not you like the so-called modern in architecture, it is responsible for more light and grace in every gimcrack building put up by tenth-rate architects than all of them together could have devised over a thousand years. Wright is the father of it, and every architect and builder should go down on his knees daily in thanks for ideas begun by him more than fifty years ago and used by people everywhere who never heard his name."

Henry said with an undertone of desperation, "As a matter of fact, Richard, I'm rather inclined to like Wright's stuff. This 'Falling Water,' for instance—"

The ringing peal of the doorbell cut him off, and the three turned their heads slowly toward the hall to see Aggie go by, to hear her quick gasp as she opened to the caller. Henry was on his feet and in the hall in a second, followed by Margaret. Warner came out of the dining room. Richard, uncertain, lingered beside his chair.

The garden was dark now, so that the figure on the lighted porch stood in huge relief against blackness.

The immense uniformed figure of Mr. Harvey, Chief of Police. Soundlessly Aggie pulled the door open, allowing him to enter, and in the crowded hall, where only Richard had not appeared, the chief's eyes met Henry's. It consumed, his entering, his seeing Henry, not above two seconds, but Margaret, clutching the door frame, thought, This is Eternity; this is what it is.

"Yes, Chief?" Henry said thickly, as though he'd forgotten how to form words.

"Now, don't get excited," Chief Harvey began, with a hand lifted to ward excitement off. "It's—"

"It's Harry!" Aggie cried in anguish. *Harry!* She clutched the navy-blue sleeve. "Is he dead? Why do you just stand there? *Is he dead?*"

"No. No, he's safe. I've got him down at the station."

"Then what's wrong?"

"Well," said the chief. He looked around unhappily. "He's killed a man."

He continued to speak, but his words, to Margaret, were as unintelligible as a voice above the surface of the water would be to one drowning. Only through the roaring around her she heard her own thin voice fly in accents of terror, "Richard! Richard . . . *where are you?*" She didn't hear him coming, but his arms were around her and she realized, blind and trembling in this haven, that only here was she safe at all, only with this support could she possibly hope to survive all the years that lay in wait.

"Then there's no question," Henry was saying, "of criminal negligence?"

"None at all, Mr. Lynch. We're making no charge.

248

There were three witnesses. It was accidental, unintentional homicide. There isn't a thing to hold him on, except that naturally we had to take him over to the courthouse for questioning. But the kid's pretty broken up, and I think if you talk to him—"

"I can try."

"He asked if you'd come down," the chief added.

"He did?" Henry hesitated, then with no indication of noticing the people he left behind, went down the steps to the waiting police car.

"You see," Chief Harvey explained, driving toward Piff's Point, "old Depew had been given notice today. Of course everybody knew it was coming, and everybody felt sorry for him, but you know yourself he was getting too old for the job." He paused. "Yes. Well, so tonight he went over there to Mills' Corners and got himself stinking. There'll be an autopsy and blood tests of course, but you can rely on it, the old man was just about unconscious. He stumbled out on the parking area there at the side of Feeney's just as young Harry backed out of his place, and three people— Feeney himself, Carey Wilkinson, you know him, and a dame, I forget her name—saw Depew stumble and take a header right under the wheels. Of course they all yelled but by that time Harry was over him, and the yelling frightened him so he bucked forward again and that did it for Gregg all right. Mashed to a—" The chief cleared his throat, pretended an interest in the dashboard. "When we got there," he resumed, "the place was in an uproar. I must say for Harry, he took it pretty good. Calm as a piece of wood." He debated that. "Well, you know what I mean."

"Wooden," Henry muttered, for some reason.

"That's it. Well, we got him over to the station and took statements from the witnesses. Feeney of course tried to deny at first the old guy was drunk as he was, but he broke down all right. This Bowles now, that was with Harry, he took a powder. Probably hitched a ride home or something. I'm going around and speak to that one tomorrow. I'll tell you something, Mr. Lynch, I was mighty surprised to see Harry in a dump like Mills' Corners. That Bowles kid, now—"

"I thought he was all right," Henry said dully.

Chief Harvey snorted. "Up to anything, to my way of thinking. But Harry— You ought"—he burst out suddenly, in the tones of a father of four—"to be more careful, Mr. Lynch."

"I know," Henry said, closing his eyes. "I know, Chief Harvey, all the things you could say to me about it."

The chief cleared his throat again. "Well . . . well, no offense meant." Henry was silent. "And none taken, I hope," the chief added. Henry shook his head. "The only thing . . . you know, of course, that Harry shouldn't have been driving after dark. He knows it too, but he won't say nothing. He's going to have his junior license revoked, there's no way out of that, and he'd better not be caught driving. Can't tell for how long. Six months, a year, maybe longer. Police magistrate will decide that. As to civil suits on the part of the family—anything like that—I don't think you'll have any trouble. First place, Gregg didn't have no family." He guffawed slightly, sobered again. "Second place, there was absolutely no negligence. Nothing to base a case on."

Henry, being driven through this nightmare, stared steadily ahead, willing the car to speed, the chief to silence. Willing, with a passionate earnestness of feeling he hadn't felt since Katherine died, for the moments to pass and leave him with his son.

"One way to look at it, I'd say," the chief droned on, "is that the old guy was just about used up anyway. Can't see where he'd have been any use to himself no more. Nor," he added pontifically, "to society. So, looked at like that, maybe Harry done him a favor," he concluded.

Henry listened incredulously. Harry, he mentally addressed his son, the chief inclines to the view that you in actuality have performed the office of Gregg's deliverer. You may look upon yourself as his dark angel of acquittance. If, as the chief says, you can look at it like that. He stirred and asked apprehensively, "You haven't said anything of this—this last—to him, have you?"

"No, no," the Chief replied. "I only give it to you as a possibility. A handle to get started with, in a manner of speaking."

"I see. Well, thank you, Chief."

"Not at all, not at all." The chief was a sincerely kind man. "I'm a father myself, Mr. Lynch, and I know how you must be feeling."

Do you? Henry thought. Yes, I suppose perhaps you do. Even a small-town policeman sees a lot of sadness, a lot of tragedy, a great many end-products of mis-understanding.

They drew up at the police station, drove down an alley, and parked at the side door, on either side of which two green lights were glowing dimly. Henry climbed stiffly out of his side of the car, walked with hanging arms and fixed eyes in the trail of the chief along a smelly hall to a room with great window blinds, green lampshades, one high desk, and a few wall benches. A solitary policeman was in charge. He'd been talking but stopped at their entrance. Harry, the only other occupant of the room, got slowly to his feet.

"Dad?" he said in a voice only slightly above a whisper. His face was colorless, his eyes wet and staring, and for a moment he held the bench to steady himself.

"Hello, son. Here I am." *Incommunicable,* Henry was saying to himself. I can't communicate with any of them. I never know what to say, never know what gesture to make, what words to use. Harry, help me. . . .

Harry said, "I'm glad you're here."

Exhaling a strangled breath, Henry crossed the room and put his arm over his son's shoulder. "Thanks," he said. And if that particular word made no sense to the policeman, it was one time when the two Lynches understood each other. "There's no need for us to wait further, is there?" Henry asked the chief. "Anything more you need can be taken care of by me or my office?"

"That'll be all right, Mr. Lynch," the chief said. "There'll be a few things but nothing that can't wait. And Harry," he added, "don't you worry about nothing. This could have been a whole lot worse, boy. A whole lot worse."

Henry, though he'd removed his arm, felt the shudder that passed through Harry, and he thought, I might have said that too. That's an adult's consolatory phrase, to say, This is bad, but how much worse it was in that other case, how much worse it could be. It occurred to him with a moving clarity that the grown-up bears shock more firmly than the child because the grown-up has standards of reference to gauge by. Even at Katherine's death he'd been able to say, "If she'd lived longer, it would have been worse." Margaret couldn't say that, so she collapsed. Harry couldn't say it, so he retreated into a moody place that only— well, that only Nan Gunning had been able to lure him out of. Oh, damn us, Henry thought. Damn our references and our thick skins and our suspicions and complacency. Damn me, because for a moment I'm seeing clearly, with humility, and even as I do I know it won't last. I used to think that once you knew a thing, you knew it always. Now I'm too old even to believe that. He felt suddenly an embracing sorrow for the whole human race, only seeing the best of itself in startled moments that flashed across the dark and disappeared.

And yet, he thought, going out of the police station with his son, we might have been denied even those flashes. Life is not an easy business, but it's what we have on this earth. It's what we have to deal with.

They drove home slowly. Now and then Henry got the impression that Harry was crying, but each time he looked diffidently in the boy's direction, Harry was staring straight through the windshield, his hands motionless in his lap.

"Harry," he said at length. "I know you'll find it difficult to credit, but you'll get over this in time. I don't mean forget it. But the—presence of it, the pressure—those will fade. Terrible things happen, son. And not always to other people. But it was an accident. You'll get over it somehow, because you have to. You do anything you have to, Harry."

He thought the boy was not going to answer. More than a mile passed before Harry turned, with just a trace of what Henry told himself strangely was a comforting smile. "Thank you, too, Dad," was all he said before turning back to the road. Henry drove on, suffocated and, in truth, embarrassed with love.

Early on Sunday morning Mr. Lynch paid a call on Mr. and Mrs. Gunning, and a little later Nan walked slowly past the pavilion, anxiously scanning the beach, already crowded.

"Here I am," said Harry, at her side.

"Oh! Oh, Harry, I didn't—" She smiled and blinked her eyes a little. "Harry, darling," she said, looking up at him with boundless love and tenderness. But she came right to the point. "How do you feel now? Are you all right?"

"I will be," he said. His face was immobile, and his eyes seemed still to be peering over a frightful abyss, but he took her hand and swung it. "Let's go over the rocks and down the beach. Maybe everyone else hasn't already thought of it."

"All right," she said eagerly. "I shouldn't sound so happy, I know. But I just am. Happy to be with you. I thought— Oh, Harry, I thought I'd never see you again."

"So did I, Nan. That's what I thought too."

And see what has brought us back together. He could not think about that though. Not with Nan, who was only glad to be with him and could never know what last night had been like. (What had last night been for Nan?) Maybe I'll never even know myself just how it was, he thought. It was vague and wavery at moments, his memory of the accident, then cruelly sharp—I have *killed* a person—then mercifully darkened again. The thing to do is try to shove it away, he told himself, shove it away for as long as I can, and then when it isn't quite so jagged, drag it out again and think it over the best way I can. Someday I shall have to think it over, only not yet.

They climbed the rocks and walked far down to the lonely, empty stretch of beach where they had been last Monday.

"Only last Monday?" he said.

"That's all," Nan told him, sinking to the sand, her legs tucked beneath her. "The foam looks like a lot of white cats on the water, doesn't it?"

"Was it—awfully bad after I left?" he asked. "I hated to beat it like that, but I couldn't see what else to do, Nan."

"There wasn't anything else. And I suppose it was bad, but just as bad for Daddy as for us." Harry's jaw tightened a little. "Oh, I know," she hurried on, "how you feel about it. But parents—they worry," she decided. "And it did look . . . peculiar." Their eyes met in remembrance.

"You're very beautiful," Harry said softly. "You were the most beautiful thing I ever saw."

For a long time they didn't speak again. They sat with their fingers clasped and only a little space between them.

Nan remembered how strange it had been to have Mr. Lynch come early in the morning, stern-faced, sad, rather supplicating, to see her parents. "I can only ask," Mr. Lynch had said. "But I ask—with all my heart." Yes, it was very queer to hear cold, withdrawn Henry Lynch speak like that for his son. And Daddy. Poor Daddy, who'd had such a hideous night (they'd all, in their house, had a hideous night), just nodded heavily when Mr. Lynch said, "I'd like to believe the children. They say the entire thing was a misunderstanding, and if they say it—"

"If they say it," Mr. Gunning had replied, "we believe it because we want so much to believe it."

"I suppose so," Henry Lynch had reflected. And then there'd been a long silence while Bert Gunning prepared to accept what he had to believe.

"All right," he'd said at last, and Nan, who'd been listening outside, caught her breath a little at the defeated voice.

"I think there's something terribly sad about grow-

ing up," she said now to Harry. "It's almost as if you
... *pushed* people out of the way so you'd have room."
When he didn't answer, she said, "Harry, are you
listening to me?"

He nodded, took a little sand and poured it into
the palm of her hand. "It's good to be with you. I can't
seem to think of anything else this morning. Only that
it's good to be with you."

"I love you, Harry. I'll love you all my life."

"Me too," he said, and they watched the sand run
out between her fingers.

ABOUT THE AUTHOR

Mary Slattery Stolz was born in Boston, Massachusetts, and grew up in New York City, where she attended Birch Wathen School, Columbia University, and the Katharine Gibbs School. She also studied at New College, North Carolina. Mrs. Stolz's first jobs included selling books at Macy's and working as a secretary at Columbia Teachers College.

As long as she can remember, Mary Stolz has loved to write. But it was not until 1950 that she submitted a manuscript for publication. TO TELL YOUR LOVE, a teen-age novel, was an immediate success.

Mrs. Stolz has written for people of all ages. Her published works include two novels and several short stories for adults, as well as many teen-age novels and books for younger children.

The author says about her writing: "Perhaps as compensation for the fact that I never learned to do figures, I discovered very early that words could be manipulated. You needn't simply read them, it was possible to move them about, choose among them, find combinations of your own, and all exactly as you pleased. That was a long time ago, but I still remember the sometimes almost unbearably exciting prospect offered by a sheet of blank paper and an idea. All through school I put words together indefatigably—verse, essays, stories, biography. I liked anything that could be written about and continued not to understand anything which needed to be figured."

Mrs. Stolz's teen-age novels include WHO WANTS MUSIC ON MONDAY?; TO TELL YOUR LOVE; THE SEA GULLS WOKE ME;

IN A MIRROR; READY OR NOT; PRAY LOVE, REMEMBER; BECAUSE OF MADELINE; GOOD-BY MY SHADOW; THE ORGANDY CUPCAKES; HOSPITAL ZONE; AND LOVE REPLIED; WAIT FOR ME, MICHAEL; and ROSEMARY.

Her books for younger children are EMMETT'S PIG, *An I Can Read Book;* FRÉDOU; THE LEFTOVER ELF; and PIGEON FLIGHT. She is the creator of the brave mice, Asa and Rambo, and their friendly enemy, Siri the cat (BELLING THE TIGER; THE GREAT REBELLION; and SIRI THE CONQUISTADOR). She is also the author of A DOG ON BARKHAM STREET (An ALA Notable Children's Book of 1960) and its companion volume, THE BULLY OF BARKHAM STREET (winner of the Nineteenth Annual Boys' Clubs of America "1964 Junior Book Award Medal").